Picture Perfect

(Wide Open Series - Book 1)

SUNDAE LEIGHTON

Picture Perfect (The Wide Open Series: Book I)

Available in these formats:

- 978-1-7350077-0-0 (Paperback)
- 978-1-7350077-1-7 (eBook AZW)
- 978-1-7350077-2-4 (eBook EPUB)

Copyright: © 2020 Sundae Leighton

All rights reserved. No part of this publication may be reproduced, distributed, or transmitted in any form or by any means, including photocopying, recording, or other electronic or mechanical methods, without the prior written permission, except in the case of brief quotations embodied in reviews and certain other non-commercial uses permitted by law.

This book is a work of fiction. Name, characters, places, incidents or otherwise are written from imagination. Any resemblance to actual person's, things, living or dead or events is coincidental.

This book is intended for mature readers 18 years and older. It contains sexually explicit and graphic scenes and language that might be offensive to some readers.

All characters in this work and all my works are 18 years of age or older.

All sexual acts are consensual.

NASCAR® and its marks are trademarks of the National Association for Stock Car Auto Racing, *LLC*.

Editing: My Brother's Editor
Cover: E. Leighton
Beta Reader: Stephanie Cooper

Chapter One
SULLY

I have absolutely *no* business being here I thought to myself as I looked around the busy NASCAR track. This was a huge mistake and I knew it. I kept telling myself on the drive up to the track that I was doing this because I needed the money and to keep that thought in my mind while I was out there sweating my ass off today. I was lucky enough to be a freelance photographer so I could take on projects like this, for companies who would pay me for my work. I normally loved shit like this, but today? Today this felt like an actual damn *job*.

I stood in the hot New England sun and pulled my dark hair into a messy bun before snapping off a couple of pictures. The drivers were getting ready to qualify for the race on Sunday and those that already had finished were standing around talking to the press and each other. I pretty much knew all of the drivers and I knew at one point or another, I was going to run into the ones that I was trying to avoid. Isn't that usually how it worked?

I used to love NASCAR racing. In fact, I used to go to as

many races as I possibly could, *when* I could, up until that fatal day that broke my heart and changed my life forever. Wait, no, scratch that. It did more than just change my life or smash my heart into a million fucking pieces, but that's at least a good place to start. My entire world was turned upside down and I had been avoiding NASCAR racing ever since that happened. I had my entire life planned out up until that day and when Cooper died? He took everything I had planned as well as my happiness with him.

"I should have stayed home," I mumbled to myself as I lifted my camera to try to get a few more pictures. Lately, I had tried to stick to babies and weddings. Again, I made a mental note to think about how I was doing this for the money and nothing more. It was nice to get out of the house for a bit and enjoy myself. Maybe I could think of this as a vacation of sorts, even if it was only a couple of hours from my house.

I spotted my friend and driver Finn Houston standing up ahead with another driver who I hadn't had the chance to meet yet. It was actually because of Finn that I heard about this job and if he hadn't pushed me to take it I most likely would be at home right now taking pictures of another *Frozen* birthday party. Nothing against Elsa or anything, but I'm just ready to *let it go*. As much as I prided myself in being a strong and independent woman, I felt a sense of relief wash over me when Finn raised his hand to wave me over.

"Hey, Sully!" Finn flashed me a big smile before he pulled me into a giant hug as soon as I got close enough. He was handsome, not as good looking as his brother Cooper had been, but close enough. He was over six feet with broad shoulders and thick dark hair. His green eyes sparkled with happiness when he pulled back to look at me. "I'm sorry I didn't get the chance to see you until now. How does it feel to be back?"

I shrugged my shoulders as I tried to think of an answer. I couldn't lie to Finn without him knowing. We knew one another too well. "It could be worse. It hasn't been as bad as I thought it would be." I let my eyes wander a bit and they landed on the driver standing next to him which turned out to be a big mistake. *Huge* mistake. I made sure to familiarize myself with some of the newer drivers once I had been hired for the job and I recognized him immediately.

Rand Shepard was not your typical race car driver. He grew up in Georgia and was around five or six years old when the racing but bit. The guy was as big as a linebacker and looked to be seven feet tall from where I stood. This was his first season of NASCAR so he might be a rookie driver, but the rumors about him being a bad boy, heartbreaker looked to be true as I watched plenty of women walk by trying to get his attention.

There was no denying Rand was attractive. The pictures I had seen did not do him justice with the inky-black hair that curled around his ears as well as the tattoos that covered his entire body. Or at least, the ones I could see with his fire suit on which was saying a lot since it covered his entire body.

Finn put his hand on Rand's shoulder. "Sully, have you met Rand yet?" He raised his eyebrows at me with a look of concern in his eyes.

I shook my head. "No, not yet." I smiled up at Rand as I

tried to ignore the alarms and bells going off in my head. Warning me to run, telling me to watch myself. I wasn't sure what it was about the young driver that had me so on edge.

"Brooklyn, right?" Rand's thick southern accent caught me off guard. His eyes were hidden behind a pair of dark sunglasses, but that didn't stop him from making me feel like he was undressing me as he slowly looked me over. A smile tugged at the corners of Rand's perfectly shaped lips and I got the feeling that he wanted to eat me alive.

I immediately hated Rand Shepard. There was no other way to describe the feeling running through my mind right now. Anger flashed through my veins as I stared up at him. Drivers like him? They thought they were every woman's dream. Cocky and so goddamn full of himself, Rand probably thought I would drop my panties for him the second he asked. Over my dead body.

"It's nice to meet you, Rand." I plastered a fake smile onto my face and turned back to Finn.

"Oh no, the pleasure is all mine, darlin'." Rand's voice shouldn't have made me feel the things I was feeling, but I couldn't seem to control my body. It was like it had a mind of its own right now. I could hear the teasing; the flirting behind his words and it took all I had not to slap him across the face just so I could wipe that smug smile from it.

Finn coughed softly. "Alright then." He shot Rand a look that might have killed him if this was a movie or television show and I was never happier to have him in my corner. "Sully, how about you take a few pictures? Rand and I would love to help you out with that."

I gritted my teeth. "That would be great, thanks." I avoided looking back in Rand's direction and instead, picked up my camera from around my neck as the two men tried to get into a more natural position. "Just relax, both of you." I giggled at the expression on Finn's face. "Just try to act normal." I clucked my tongue along the roof of my mouth. "If that's possible." I shot a look at Rand for a second just so he knew that yes, dickhead, I was talking to you.

"Darlin'." Rand's smooth southern accent washed over me like butter on toast. "I couldn't be more natural if I tried." I resisted the urge to tell him to shove it up his ass and instead, plastered that fake smile back on my face. I needed this job. I needed this money. London, she needed to stay in school.

Finn shot a look over at Rand. "Dude, you're acting like a real douche. We talked about this." His eyes had gone hard. "Knock it the fuck off."

Haha, I wanted to laugh at him. Finn, forever my protector and for a second I felt a wave of heartache wash over me like I hadn't felt in a very long time. Cooper and Finn, shit, they were the best bodyguards a girl could ask for until—.

"Sully?" Finn brought me back to reality.

I looked up at the sound of my name. "Sorry." I turned to face Finn and Rand but had to take a step back. Rand had removed those dark sunglasses and staring back at me now were a pair of the bluest eyes I had ever seen. They were so blue you might think you could swim in them and for a moment I swore that he could see straight into my soul. Shame and desire mingled deep in my throat as heat settled deep in my belly. Fuck me.

I gathered myself together and managed to snap off a few shots of Finn and Rand together before I got a couple of each, alone. I knew that I was working faster than I normally did and I hated myself for it. I tried to shrug it off with the excuse that I could see how tired they both were, how tired *I* was, and the fact that I wanted to try to get ahold of London tonight if possible. I wanted to make sure she was doing alright and just wanted to hear her voice. I hated having her so far away, but she was happy and doing what she loved. We both were.

The real reason I was moving so fast was because I wanted to get away from Rand Shepard as fast as I could. I didn't like him or trust him.

"Thanks." I covered the lens of my camera when I was finished. "Appreciate your help." I met Finn's gaze and he smiled at me. "Good luck this weekend," I added as an afterthought.

"Text me later, Sully." Finn pulled me into a hug again and I knew he meant well. I also knew he would try to drag me out to some party that I didn't want to be at. He let go of me and glanced over at his teammate who was unzipping his fire suit.

"Don't need luck," Rand stated and when I turned to look at him I instantly regretted it. "I could, however, use the company of a beautiful woman. Any plans tonight, darlin'?"

My mouth fell open as I stared up at him. Motherfucker, who did this guy think he was? I noticed the way his white undershirt clung to his broad, chiseled chest and the colorful tattoos that were visible now. "Excuse me?" I managed to stammer out.

"Come on, Brooklyn." Rand took a step toward me, and I took one back. ""I don't see a ring on that pretty little hand of yours, so unless you have a boyfriend back home—"

My entire body began to shake. I wasn't entirely sure if it was because I was angry or excited about the words coming out of Rand's mouth right now.

"That's enough, Shepard." Finn stepped between us before I had the chance to do something I really shouldn't. Or say something even worse.

I watched as a huge smile broke out on Rand's face. A smile so bright that it would put the Rockefeller Christmas tree to shame. "Alright, no need to get so upset." He ran a hand through his hair. "I'm sorry if I upset you, darlin'." He still had that shit-eating grin on his face that made me not want to trust him. "But, if you change your mind, you know where to find me."

"You." Finn gave Rand a little shove. "Need to chill the fuck out and go back to your RV. Take a cold shower or something. What the fuck?"

Rand didn't look one bit sorry about what he said. He shook his head at me before turning and leaving me standing there with Finn who looked absolutely madder than a wet hornet. "Sully—"

"I'm fine." I put my hand up. I'll be fine. I have a few more pictures I need to try to get before I head back to my hotel. Don't worry, I'm a survivor, remember?"

Finn looked like he wanted to say something more, but he didn't. "Text me. Just let me know you're alright."

I assured him I would and we both went our separate ways. I realized that I wanted *nothing* to do with Rand Shepard and I was going to make sure as hell I stayed away from him the rest of the weekend.

Little did I know that wasn't going to be the case.

Chapter Two
RAND

I couldn't seem to get that cute little brunette out of my mind. She wasn't the typical woman I went after. I was more of the blonde hair, big tits kind of guy, but I couldn't help but give Brooklyn a hard time. Shit, she had tried so hard to come across as *not* interested in me that I knew she had to be.

Finn had made me promise to leave her alone, told me she was off-limits and not available. I wanted to tell him I didn't see a ring on her finger, which had never stopped me before, but the look on his face was so serious I thought he might actually hit me. Sure, Finn was a good dude. But we weren't super close or anything. He wasn't my best friend.

So, when Finn came banging on my RV door forty-five minutes ago and asked me to do him a solid or rather, Brooklyn, I was kind of caught off guard. Seemed the little firecracker had gone and told Travis Kerr that she had a date with yours truly tonight.

Let me back that up a bit. Travis, a fellow NASCAR driver, was having a get-together tonight with a bunch of other guys and apparently invited Brooklyn. I guess that he had a thing for her from way back, I couldn't blame the guy, and she had had a reason to blow him off in the past. Until now. But, this time she went ahead and said she had a date with me. Which I found completely hilarious.

"Wait a second." I grinned at Finn. I couldn't believe what he had just told me. "Tell me again what she said?" I folded my arms across my chest and leaned against the door frame.

Finn shifted his weight from one foot to the other. "You heard me the first time, Shepard. Can you help Sully out or not?" The look in his eyes was hard to figure out and I hadn't had the balls to ask him what their deal was. Yet.

"I think I remember you telling me to stay away from her?" I reminded him. "She also made it pretty clear that she wasn't interested in me so why would she tell Travis she had a date with me?" I chuckled softly.

"Look." Finn narrowed his eyes at me. "I can't answer that, you'll have to ask Sully that question. Can you please help her out? Go with her to the damn party and leave after an hour. Fuck it, thirty minutes for all I care. Do it for me, man."

"Fine." I was going to say yes anyway because even though I could handpick a dozen girls, Brooklyn Sullivan was the one I couldn't seem to stop thinking about right now. "Tell her to wear something nice," I added and saw anger flare up in Finn's eyes. "I'm kidding!" Jesus, did he have a thing for her? If he did, all Finn had to do was tell me and I would back off.

"Take a damn shower and put on something clean and simple. I'll go tell Sully you'll go with her. Don't be a fucking asshole tonight." Finn glared at me. "I fucking mean it. I'll be back within an hour." He looked like he might say something else, but instead turned and stomped out of my RV.

It wasn't a date or at least a real one, but I dressed like it was anyway. After my shower, I put on a polo shirt that had my sponsors' logo on it and a fresh pair of black jeans. I liked my hair the way it was these days even though it was a little longer than most of the other drivers'. Then again, I wasn't like most of the other drivers and I liked to remind everyone of that. I was six foot five which made me taller than they were. I worked out as much as I could so I was solid muscle and I was completely covered in tattoos.

See? Different. I liked it that way, too.

I slipped my wallet into one pocket and my cell into the other before I heard Finn outside again, but I could hear Brooklyn out there, too. I squared my shoulders and opened the door. I had been kidding when I said I wanted her to look nice, but she was wearing a little green dress that made my cock swell and stand at attention so much it hurt. She looked downright sexy. I stepped outside and immediately started sweating which caused me to wonder if it was the warm summer night or the woman standing in front of me.

Brooklyn smiled up at me, her face looking fresh and clean, except for a slight tint of lip gloss on her pouty lips. "I appreciate you helping me out tonight, Rand." Her dark hair was no longer pulled back and I noticed it was so long that it almost touched her ass. Twitch. There went my cock again.

"I'll leave you two." Finn's eyes were glued to me like I was some sort of serial killer. "Have fun and *behave*." He hugged Brooklyn, but narrowed his eyes at me again like I was Ted Bundy. Like I was planning on riding off in my Volkswagen Beetle and someone would find her body on the side of the road tomorrow morning.

I hadn't even said a word yet. I was too busy ogling Brooklyn and staring at the way her dress hugged her waist and the way her small tits were pushed together just showing off enough cleavage to be classy, but not slutty. Shit, I shouldn't have agreed to this. I wasn't the type of guy to just go on a date with a woman, and not bang her.

"Listen." Brooklyn put her hand on my arm and it was like a jolt of electricity right through my veins. I'm pretty sure she felt it, too, because she pulled her hand off me faster than the babysitter's boyfriend when the parents' car pulls up. She didn't seem to miss a beat though. "We'll go to the party and stay for about a half hour or so. Then you go off and do whatever you had originally planned for your Saturday night."

I usually had a girl waiting for me, but tonight for some reason I didn't. Not for the lack of trying, because I had with Brooklyn, but she shot me down so fast I hadn't had time to try another one. I think I was going numb with her warm little hand on my arm because I couldn't even begin to think about anything else.

"Sure, no problem," I mumbled like some sort of stupid kid who was talking to his high school crush. I didn't trust myself to say anything else at this point because my brain was thinking about Brooklyn's lips wrapped around my cock or her soft skin pressed against my chest.

Shit. Fuck. Crap.

"Should, should we go?" Brooklyn glanced up at me and when she started walking I managed to start moving with her. She started talking again but I'll be damned if I could tell you about what.

Fuck, I was getting hard and I should have been focusing on what Brooklyn was saying. I might have been a playboy kind of guy, but I *was* the kind of date that liked to actually listen to what his date was saying when they were out together. I wasn't a *complete* prick. I stared at her profile as we got into her little blue Ford and thought about what her legs would feel like wrapped around my waist. Dammit. I was doing it again.

Brooklyn kept glancing at me while she was talking and I'm pretty sure she noticed the bulge in my pants. I mean, it was pretty obvious. But, she just kept on talking. Maybe she thought I was just being that asshole again from earlier, the one that had hit on her. Or maybe she was just trying to be chatty and get this whole thing over with so she could go back to her hotel room and do whatever it is she did when she wasn't taking pictures. Call her boyfriend. Or girlfriend. I don't judge.

Or, maybe I was making Brooklyn nervous. The thought made me feel a little bit more like myself and I felt a little sense of relief wash over me. Who the fuck was I right now? I watched as she pulled her car into the restaurant parking lot and we both climbed out of the car.

Brooklyn turned to me outside the door before we went inside.

"Don't take this the wrong way, but Travis is a fucking asshole."

I laughed. I couldn't help it. She was right; even though I liked Travis he had this sort of arrogance about him. Some drivers got that way. Seriously, the guy rented out an entire restaurant so that he could celebrate his own fucking birthday. Who does that sort of thing?

"He annoys me sometimes. He drives great and I'm sure in time will be racing with the best of them. I thanked you before and I'll thank you again for coming here with me tonight," Brooklyn told me.

I leaned forward and opened the door letting Brooklyn go inside before me. "I'm glad I could help, darlin'." I smiled as she walked inside. Pretend date or not, I was going to try to make the best of it.

Chapter Three
RAND

The place was already packed when we stepped inside. I noticed a few drivers with their significant others. Most of them were too busy eating and drinking to pay much attention to us, but I saw them all. I cared about what they thought even though I pretended not to. I saw Finn sitting in the back with the Wagner brothers, and I caught the way he was watching me, his eyes telling me if I fucked this up he'd make me suffer.

"There's a spot." Brooklyn turned slightly to catch my eye and started forwarded just as we both saw Travis heading toward us.

I'm not sure what came over me but the fucker had this look on his face. Maybe the same look I usually wore, but I dropped my arm over Brooklyn's shoulder like she belonged to me and I felt her body grow stiff underneath me. Travis immediately stopped in his tracks and stared at us like a complete creeper.

I couldn't help but smirk at him as we made our way over to the booth and I let Brooklyn sit down first. Yep, I was absolutely feeling more like myself. I slipped into the seat across from her and grabbed the waitress's attention to order us a couple of drinks.

Brooklyn was staring at me like I had grown three heads and gills. She placed her arms on the table and laced her fingers together. "You know this isn't a real date, right?" she hissed at me.

I broke into a smile. "Darlin', it's a date, real or not." I looked up as the waitress materialized next to us. "I'll have a Bud." I glanced back at Brooklyn.

"I'm driving. I'll take a water." She nearly growled out her order.

"I need to see an ID," the waitress told me. Her name tag said Brittney, but she looked more like a Delores or Hilda. She was probably my mother's age if I had to guess, with caked-on makeup and overly teased blonde hair that desperately needed a touch-up by the looks of the roots growing in.

"Come on now." I flashed my famous smile. "Do we really have—"

"I know who you are and it's an ID or no beer." Brittney smacked her lips together. "It's super busy tonight, Rand. I don't have time for your bullshit," she added to let me know she really *did* know who I was.

"Coke." I rolled my eyes. "Nachos, too, if you have them," I added as an afterthought. My eyes were back on my date and she had a surprised look on her face and I realized she didn't know I was eight years younger than she was. "I'm twenty, not that age matters." I watched as her eyes grew round.

"Jesus." Brooklyn started chewing on her bottom lip which made me want to suck on it. Her eyes moved around the restaurant before she looked back at me. "Tell me about yourself." She leaned against the back of the booth. "It's not a date, but you could make it look like one, please, Rand."

"It's your typical driver story." I looked at the curve of her neck and wanted to find the spot that drove her crazy. Kiss and bite it. All women had one. I began to tell Brooklyn my usual story, the one the media already knew. "I grew up racing in Georgia, did the usual dirt track, midget shit. It was in my blood as soon as I could walk. I loved cars and couldn't get enough of them."

Brooklyn was twirling a piece of hair between her fingers when Brittney came back with our drinks and said the food would be up in a few minutes. "Your family?" she asked before taking a sip of her water.

"I'm an only child." I watched the way her lips wrapped around the straw and my cock strained against my jeans. Fuck me, if that wasn't the sexiest thing I had seen all night. "My parents come to as many races as they can, but they work, too." Lies, lies, lies. But what did Brooklyn know?

"Isn't this some cute and cozy shit." Travis suddenly dropped down next to me in the booth. "Shepard, my man, how did you do it?" He slung his arm around the back of the booth, and around my shoulders. Dude, we aren't even close to being friends and he knew it.

"Travis," Brooklyn started to interrupt him.

"No, come on. I want to know. Look, I know you've had a

rough go of it the past few years since Cooper died and I *get* that, Sully. If anything, we all figured you'd end up with Finn, but Shepard?" Travis stunk of booze. His eyes were red and his words slurred when he spoke. I wondered how much he had already had to drink tonight.

The look on Brooklyn's face was enough to break anyone's heart. I knew about Cooper Houston. Everyone in the racing community did. Finn's older brother had nearly been a NASCAR champion until he was killed in a car crash before the end of the season. I knew he had had a fiancée, I just didn't know it was Brooklyn.

"If you just needed a little dick, Sully, I could have helped you with that. A real man, not a little boy." Travis laughed like he was the funniest man on the planet.

I didn't remember it happening or how it started, but the next thing I knew, I had Travis on the floor of the restaurant and I was on top of him. Hitting him. Over and over and over again. I wasn't the type of guy to do shit like that. I didn't usually start fights and I certainly didn't get into them. I did, however, believe in respecting women.

"Rand!" Brooklyn's voice sounded far away. So very far away and I felt like maybe I was in a dream. "Rand, stop it, please!"

I looked up and she was looking at me, no pleading with me, and I looked down to see what I was doing. "Holy fuck." It looked like maybe I had broken Travis's nose. I was bigger than him, but I didn't do as much damage as I could have. I jumped to my feet and noticed everyone was watching me. "I didn't—"

Brooklyn was standing next to Finn and he had her in a half hug. Why did I fucking do that? She wasn't my girlfriend. She didn't even *like* me.

"Are you fucking crazy?" Travis managed to get to his feet. "What the fuck is *wrong* with you?"

I was going to hit him again if I didn't get out of here. "Leave her alone," I grunted. "I fucking mean it, Travis." I pushed past everyone else and nearly knocked the door off its hinges making my way outside. The air was humid still, but at least I was free from prying eyes. I was going insane, that would explain it.

"Rand?"

I turned around to find Brooklyn's big doe eyes staring up at me. "Look I know I had no fucking right to do that and it's none of my business. I'll—" I couldn't breathe when she threw herself at me. Literally threw herself into my arms and hugged me with her tiny little body.

"Thank you," Brooklyn whispered, but I heard her. Her scent was intoxicating. Like peaches and vanilla and I was afraid if I hugged her back I would break. Not break her. Break myself after building myself up. But when she started crying? I cracked, just a little.

I wrapped my arms around her as much as I would allow myself. "Darlin', don't cry. I'm sure that any good man would do that for you." Which I am not, but I can pretend to be. "It's alright." I rubbed Brooklyn's back with my hand.

"You made a fucking mess in there, Shepard." Finn's voice broke the mood and Brooklyn pulled away. That fucker was like a goddamn yeast infection that wouldn't go away. "Nice job."

I turned around. "*Fuck. You.*" I wanted to shove him. Something in me had snapped. "I didn't *ask* for this. You asked me to help and I did. I was just defending Brooklyn. Something I didn't see you doing." Shit. Shit. Fuck. Words I shouldn't say and yet there they were. I looked over at Brooklyn and she looked like shit, I couldn't figure it out.

"How about I drive you back to the hotel, Sully? Shepard can take my truck back to the track and in the morning I'll pick you up." Finn ignored me. I was used to that.

Say no. Please say no. Drive me back so I can talk to you alone and I'll explain everything. I silently begged her.

"It's okay, Finn." Brooklyn sighed. "I'll drive him." One point to Shepard, she picked me fucker. I wanted to gloat but kept it to myself.

Finn opened his mouth but then closed it. I saw it then, clear as fucking day. He was in love with Brooklyn. Whether she knew it or not I wasn't sure, but he was, and I felt bad for the guy. Maybe. "Be careful." He didn't say anything else as he went back inside. Probably to try to clean up my mess. Which I was going to have to deal with tomorrow. Brooklyn looked at me and then started walking so I followed her. It had a different feel than just a little while ago when we arrived. Less fun and more serious. When I climbed into the car I watched as she put the key into the ignition and I put my hand over her wrist.

"I don't want to end things like this—" I managed to tell her. "I'm not that kind of man, darlin'."

"What kind of man?" Brooklyn looked down at my hand

before she met my eyes. Her eyes were sad and I didn't like it.

I stole the kiss before Brooklyn could stop me, our lips meeting in a hot, wet slide. Her lips were warm and welcoming, her tongue meeting mine. I kissed Brooklyn again and again, trying to make the world go away. I would have kept going if she didn't pull away.

"I'm sorry..." Tears spilled down her cheeks.   "I can't."

I turned her face to look at me. "You don't have to do anything you don't want to, Brooklyn. It was a kiss," I reminded her. "Nothing more."

Brooklyn nodded and started the car without another word. I knew I fucked up. I shouldn't have hit Travis. And I absolutely shouldn't have kissed her. I was glad the ride back to the track was short and when we got back I jumped out of the car as fast as I could.

"Thanks. I mean, whatever." I didn't know what I was saying or why I was saying it. I needed a drink, which I had back at my RV. "I'll see you around." I didn't even wait for her to answer me. I just started walking and when I got back to my RV I kicked off my shoes and pulled off my shirt before digging a beer out of my refrigerator. I popped the top off and nearly drank the whole thing before there was a knock at the door.

I hoped it wasn't Finn. Or Travis. Or the cops. Fuck.

I opened the door and found Brooklyn standing there.

"Can I come in?"

Chapter Four
SULLY

Everything seemed to happen so damn fast. Rand hitting Travis and then I was thanking him. Hugging him even and I didn't even like him. Yet, I let the man kiss me in the car and it did things to me. Things that I hadn't felt in such a long time and maybe it was because I missed Cooper or maybe it was because I missed being with a man, but I was standing outside Rand's door right now.

I knew it was wrong. *So* wrong.

Rand was young, so very young, and I was this tortured soul that he saved just for one night. He was this bad boy that slept with whoever he wanted and didn't try to hide it. He wasn't what I needed.

Yet, I still knocked on the door.

Rand looked just as surprised as I did when he opened the door. When I saw him standing there in just his jeans, his thick muscled chest beckoning to me with all those tattoos, I nearly ran.

But I didn't.

"Can I come in?" My body felt like it wasn't mine right now. Pleasure pulsed in my blood as I waited for his answer.

Rand pushed the screen door open without a word and stepped back so I could enter his RV. I could feel his blue eyes burning into me as I glanced around the darkened kitchen area before turning back to face him. He had moved closer. So close that I could smell the scent of exhaust and gasoline on his skin.

"Rand—" I took a step back and felt the counter against my back causing my breath to hitch in my throat.

His bright eyes had turned dark with desire. "What are you doing here, Brooklyn? You don't belong here." Rand's thick accent sent shivers up my spine and my pussy clamped down around itself.

The man was beautiful, a fantasy come to life. Rand had a hard, muscled body and all I could think about was what it would feel like lying underneath him. With him inside me. Fuck, I was in trouble. "You left in such a hurry and I wanted to see you again." It wasn't a lie.

Rand's hand came up and touched my neck with the tips of his fingers. "I'm no good for you, darlin'. Whatever you're looking for, I'm not it." His arm slipped down around my waist as he pulled me against his hard chest. "I'll ask you again. What are you doing here?" He pressed his lips against the curve of my neck causing my nipples to become hard pebbles under the fabric of my bra. His tongue flicked back and forth while he continued his vampire-like action before he bit down softly.

A soft moan escaped my lips before I could stop it. Rand grabbed my hair and tangled it into a makeshift ponytail as he pinned me against the wall.

"I can make you forget, Brooklyn. I can make you feel things you've never felt before, but I can't be what you really need." Fire raced from Rand's body as he pressed against me. "I'm no one's boyfriend. I'm not husband material. I need you to understand that."

"I'm not very experienced." I needed Rand to understand *that*. I had only been with Cooper and I didn't think that counted as much.

"Darlin'." Rand's lips were inches from mine, his voice causing liquid to leak from my pussy like a faucet. "I'll take care of everything." He released my hair before taking a step back. "Beer?" He reached back behind him and held it out. "I was just going to have another one before you stopped by."

I was confused. What the fuck?

Rand walked over to the silver refrigerator and pulled out two bottles. He placed both on the counter before popping one open. He took a swig out of one and turned those blues on me. "Take off your dress."

"What?" I blinked at him.

"Take off your dress, darlin'." Rand put the bottle down on the counter and unbuttoned his jeans. "You look fucking banging in that thing, but something tells me you'll look better without it on." His lips turned up slightly. "Do you need help?" He stepped toward me.

"N-no." I shook my head and slipped off my shoes before looking back up at him. Christ, he was a giant of a man. I eased my dress down, letting it fall to the floor without looking away. I felt so exposed standing there in just my bra and panties, Rand's eyes raking over me.

"Can I ask you a question? It might be a little personal." Rand tilted his head and when I nodded, he went on. "Is Cooper the only guy you ever fucked?"

If anyone else had asked me that question I would have slapped them. Or screamed at them. Rand, on the other hand? That was something I would have expected from him.

"Yes," I whispered and felt tears fill my eyes. "I don't want to talk about him." Rand's lips were on mine again. Hard and demanding. Hot and wet. I met his kisses with my own. Open-mouthed and panting he helped me to the couch without me even realizing it until my head hit the cushion behind me.

Rand was hard with arousal for *me*. I could feel his cock pressed against my stomach as our tongues fought together inside my mouth. I wanted to touch him, and I rubbed against him eagerly, like a horny teenager. It had been so long, too long. My sex was pounding and aching to be filled.

Rand chuckled softly but when he ran his fingers down my underwear he growled deep in his chest. I knew my underwear was completely wet, they had been the moment I saw him half naked in the doorway. My hips bucked against Rand's touch, my clit desperate and ready.

"You're going to come the fucking second I touch you," Rand murmured and I closed my eyes when he rubbed his hand against my pussy. I was already quivering and trembling, ready to explode on impact. "No. That's not going to work with me. Look at me, darlin'. Look at me when I make you come."

I opened my eyes to find Rand watching me, eyes hooded with heat. Then he pushed my cotton underwear back and flicked at my wet clit with his thick finger. Once. Twice. I exploded on Rand on the third try, my body crippled with pleasure. I felt dizzy with desire when I cried out his name enjoying the feeling that pulsed between my legs. I felt strange and somewhat ashamed when my climax was over, unsure of what had just happened.

"Wipe that look off your face." Rand shook his head. "You did nothing wrong, Brooklyn."

I sat up and moved closer. I had never been very good at oral with Cooper, but I would try my best for Rand. He had hardly even touched me and I had gone off like a rocket. I placed my hand over his impressive bulge.

"This was about you—shit, fuck." Rand's breath caught in his throat when I squeezed him lightly. He watched as I started to unzip his jeans with shaky hands.

Impressive bulge. Impressive cock. I didn't have much to compare it to. Cooper was probably average size from what I'd seen. Rand wasn't wearing any underwear which didn't seem to surprise me. His dick popped out hard and veiny like a porn cock. It stood at attention and pulsed with the beat of his heart. I climbed between his legs to get a better angle and ran my hand up the shaft.

I was surprised at how soft the skin was. At the sounds Rand made deep in his chest when I made a fist around his dick. I was unsure of myself but I knew I wanted to make him feel good. Rand was watching. Waiting for my next move.

"Lick it, darlin'. It won't hurt you." His accent. Shit, it was sexy. His hands moved to my hair when I dropped my mouth down to his cock and when he fisted them into my hair, I slowly ran my tongue up his cock tracing the vein I saw running from his balls to the tip. "Shit… that's it." He groaned and pulled me closer. "Don't be afraid of it." Rand tightened his hold on me. "As long as you don't use teeth, we're golden."

I gripped the base of Rand's cock and lowered my head to take him in my mouth. I moved slowly, trying to get a feel of what I was doing. Letting the muscles of my jaw get used to the feel of his member. I sucked hard and tried to force myself to take him as deep as I could. The taste of Rand's flesh was sweaty, but I liked it. So much so that once again my underwear was damp with want. Something that I had never anticipated. It was usually a one and done type of situation with Cooper.

"Fuck, darlin'. You look beautiful sucking my cock right now," Rand whispered, arching his hips toward my mouth. "I'm going to come." He moaned and tugged on my hair.

I ate it up like it was my last meal. Hot and salty, Rand's seed filled my mouth and I swallowed every drop as he blurted out obscenities.

Another first for me tonight. Go me.

Rand pulled me back up onto the couch and onto his lap, his blues searching mine before I kissed him. I felt him tugging on the cups of my bra and running his hands over my hard nipples as our mouths tore at one another. Rand tugged on my underwear and managed to peel them off leaving me naked from the waist down.

"Condom." It came out in a moan. I wanted this so badly, but I wasn't stupid.

Rand's hand reached next to him on the table and I heard the ripping of the package before he moved to slip it on. "Always prepared," he teased me. "Okay?" His cock was already hard again.

I bit my lip and straddled Rand's waist. I slowly started to bear down on him and I swore I was going to come again. Just from that alone. "Rand," I whimpered as my muscles clenched and rippled around him.

Holy fuck.

Rand pulled me against his muscled chest and I bit down on his shoulder. My orgasm hit me by surprise as I felt his cock drag across my swollen clit. But when Rand shouted out my name and I felt his body tense up underneath me, the second orgasm ripped through me like an ocean wave. I slumped against him like my body was made out of jelly.

Staying the night was something I shouldn't do. If someone saw me in the morning, I could only imagine the rumors. Like there wouldn't be enough already.

"You can stay." Rand's soft whisper shook me from the sex haze sleep I was drifting into.

I moved off of his legs. "I shouldn't—"

Rand kissed the side of my mouth. "Darlin', I'm not asking you to move in with me. It's late." He was already standing up and holding out his hand. "I won't let a woman sleep on the couch either. Come on, the bed is big enough for two."

Bells. Alarms. Whistles.

Warning me again.

Run as fast as you can, girl.

But I didn't, and I took Rand's hand, letting him lead me to his bedroom.

Chapter Five
RAND

Brooklyn tried to sneak out of my RV. I almost let her go. I almost wish I had. First rule I had about fucking women? Don't, **DON'T** let them sleep over and **DON'T** let them sleep in your bed. **DON'T** sleep in theirs. This wasn't a sleepover.

That shit was for kids.

I couldn't let Brooklyn do the walk of shame though. She was too good for that. I didn't sleep much with her scent surrounding me. That shit was intoxicating. Dangerously so. I watched her sleeping next to me, her dark curls spread out on the pillow. I resisted the urge to touch her.

But, fuck if I hadn't wanted to.

I watched Brooklyn's eyelids flutter and wondered what she was dreaming about. Her lips smacked together and instantly my cock responded. Memories of her mouth wrapped around me made me harden in a second and I thought about how her underwear had been so fucking wet when I touched them. How she had just exploded when she slipped down my shaft. I did, too, now that I thought about it.

Brooklyn rolled onto her side while she slept. She was fucking beautiful, a petite wisp of a woman with porcelain skin. Those big chestnut-brown eyes and that hair. That gorgeous mane of hair. I reached over and wrapped a ringlet around my finger before I could stop myself.

I hadn't meant to fuck her. When I opened the door last night and saw Brooklyn standing there looking all innocent and wide-eyed, I knew exactly what she wanted. What she *needed*. Rules were meant to be broken.

Right?

Suddenly, Brooklyn gasped and sat up like she realized she wasn't where she was supposed to be. Bad dream maybe? Her eyes swept around the darkened room and I quickly shut my eyes so she didn't think I was some sort of creep. Then I heard her slip off the bed and tiptoe out of the room.

That's when I realized she was going to sneak out. Either Brooklyn realized she made a mistake or she wanted to get out before anyone saw her.

I didn't let her go though. I grabbed my jeans off the floor, managing to pull them up enough so I could follow her. Brooklyn had stripped off the shirt I had given her to sleep in and had slipped on her green dress from last night.

I flipped on the light. "Going somewhere, darlin'?" I felt a lazy smile spread across my face as I leaned against the doorway.

Brooklyn dropped her shoes like she was stealing them. "Rand!" I watched the color creep up her neck and over her face. "I was, well—" She watched me as I moved slowly across the room and pressed start on the coffee machine. "I was leaving. It's probably best if I go before anyone sees me coming out of your RV."

I leaned casually against the counter this time. "You thought you'd leave without telling me? Isn't that kind of something I'd do?" I was trying to be a dick about it. Trying to push Brooklyn away in hopes she'd go back to hating me. It was something I was used to. I would only end up breaking her in the end.

"Why are you looking at me like I did something wrong? We both know I shouldn't have stayed here." Brooklyn narrowed her eyes at me. "Why *did* you let me stay here?"

The coffee finished so I grabbed a couple of mugs. "Coffee?" I poured the hot drink into both cups and turned to face Brooklyn again. "I know you hate me, darlin'." I grabbed the sugar out of the cabinet and dumped a couple of packets into my coffee. "But, I'm not a complete asshole. I wasn't about to let a beautiful woman go out in the dark in the middle of the night by herself."

"I don't hate you," Brooklyn mumbled.

There was something about the petite brunette that made my blood grow hot. That made me want to crush her body against mine. "You should hate me." I smirked into my coffee. "I already told you I'm not the boyfriend type."

"I don't want a boyfriend," Brooklyn hissed at me. Sadness suddenly weighed heavily in the room and it was her grief. "Coffee's getting cold." I turned away so Brooklyn couldn't see the shame I suddenly felt. "Can I have the sugar?"

Brooklyn's soft voice was to the left of me and when I looked over at her, I saw the contempt in her eyes. It spilled out of her like an open wound. Achievement unlocked. She was pissed at me again.

I slid it across the counter without a word and watched as she dropped two packets into her coffee before taking a sip. The knock at the door surprised us both. The sun wasn't even up yet—never mind the rest of the world. Who in the fuck would be at my door this early? I moved to unlock the door, but only pulled it back enough so I could see who was there.

Well, shit.

Finn looked like he hadn't slept at all. I mean, *at all*. "Have you seen Sully?" His eyes were bloodshot, his clothes a rumpled mess. Those looked exactly like his clothes from last night. "Either you let me inside or I make my way inside." His voice sounded very un-Finn like, too.

I pushed the door back so Finn could come inside. I was never good at secrets anyway. I had a shitty poker face and I didn't want to hide anything. Of course he knew she was here. I made sure of that. I had a couple of guys I considered friends in NASCAR and I had made sure they told a couple of guys, who told a couple of guys *exactly* where Brooklyn was last night. And with who.

Finn looked confused at first. I guess love can make you do stupid shit. Or so I've been told. "Sully?" His voice cracked. "What's going on?" Finn looked between the two of us. "You were supposed to bring Shepard home. Did-did you *fuck* him?" He began to laugh hysterically. "This is fucking perfect, Sully. Of all the goddamn people." He clenched his fists at his side. "Un-fucking-believable."

"Back the fuck off, man," I warned Finn. I might sleep with a lot of women, but I respected them.

Finn caught me by surprise when he shoved me. It was enough so that I stumbled backward. "You! You were supposed to be my friend!"

I pushed him back. I was bigger. Stronger. I made sure of that. Finn's arms went out when he tried to catch himself, but he crashed backward against the door. I watched the hate blaze through him. "I never said I was your friend, Finn."

"Stop it!" Brooklyn shouted. If she cared for either of us, she gave no sign of it. "I'm not a child." She jutted her chin out. "Stop treating me like some sort of helpless idiot." Her gaze was cold when it settled on me. "Both of you."

"Sully—" Finn stood up.

Brooklyn shook her head. "Finn. I'm an adult. Yes, I slept with Rand and I'm sorry if that upset you. It doesn't mean I don't love Cooper. But, I need to start living my life again. You have to learn to give me some space." She crossed her arms over her chest. "I'm not mad at you, Finn."

Finn poked me in the chest as his face twisted with anger. "You're dead to me, Shepard." He looked like he wanted to say more, but instead he stomped out of my RV and slammed the door behind him.

Well, fuck me sideways. Guess I won't be sending him a Christmas card this year.

I ran my hand over the back of my neck and squeezed it. I

looked at Brooklyn, who was glaring at me. "Go on, darlin'. Give it to me. I can handle it." I let a cocky grin spread across my face knowing it would piss her off even more.

"You are fucking unbelievable!" Brooklyn erupted. The slap I didn't see coming. Her hand came up fast and hit me hard. Just once, although I'm sure she wanted to hit me a few more times. "That man—" Her eyes were black with hate now. "He has done so much for me. Could you have maybe lied to him? You fucking broke him."

"I'm not a liar, darlin'. Sometimes people have to see the truth in order to move forward." I sat down on one of the kitchen chairs. "Guessing you understand that now."

"You—" Brooklyn looked ready to spit nails right about now. "You're... I don't know what you are!" She glared at me and then moved to grab her shoes from the floor. "I'm done with you." She shoved her feet inside her heels. "Please don't try to contact me."

"Wouldn't dream of it, darlin'." I raised my eyebrows at her. "You knew who I was when you came here last night." The sudden need to touch her was overwhelming and I resisted the urge to sit on my own hands. "I'll see you around."

"Like hell," Brooklyn grunted. "Don't... never mind." She whipped open the door. "Goodbye, Rand." She didn't slam the door like Finn did.

I jumped up off the chair so I could watch Brooklyn go. I had already broken so many rules with this girl, so why not a couple more? She moved like a dream across the grass and part of me was begging her to stop. Hoping that Brooklyn would turn around and what? Come back to my RV? Well fuck. She didn't though and my heart might have actually hurt. Just a little bit.

I liked Brooklyn Sullivan. That was a big fucking problem.

Happy goddamn race day, you filthy motherfucking animal.

Chapter Six
SULLY

I decided to bail on the race.

I went back to the hotel and tried to get more sleep. After tossing and turning for a couple of hours, I finally got up and decided to just go home. I would avoid so many issues that way. I could deal with Finn later. I wouldn't have to see Travis again. And, Rand? Well, I wouldn't have to see him again either.

I made up an excuse about not feeling well. That the heat had been bothering me and that I felt like I might pass out. I was, after all, my own boss. I was going to get paid for the pictures I took on Saturday and that would be enough. I hoped it would be enough.

I'm a shitty sister.

I knew what I was getting into when I went to Rand. I knew who he was. Such a fucking asshole. That's what he was. What he *is*. Why couldn't he have just lied to Finn instead of letting him into the RV this morning? Not that there was anything going on between us.

I slept with Rand Shepard. I let him fuck me. Well, alright.

If you wanted to get technical, I fucked him. I gave him a blow job and I swallowed his cum. I swore I didn't like him and yet I couldn't seem to stop thinking about him.

Rand had told me... Had *warned* me...that he wasn't the boyfriend type. He didn't date. That's why I went to him in the first place. It had been so damn long since I had been with a man and he just seemed like the man I needed to get the job done.

Fuck. Shit. Crap.

Okay, sure. He was hot. I mean, the tattoos were a plus. And he had a nice body, right? Maybe I should call my best friend, Harper Rose, on my way back home. No. No, I couldn't do that. She'd just pump me for questions about Rand's dick and that wasn't any of her business. I mean, I'd share a little bit of information with her. But that would be later.

Rand's dick was nice though. Dammit. I felt my pussy start to pound at the thought of his cock and what it looked like. How it had felt. This was not good. I had told Rand to stay away from me. I meant it, too.

I was getting all sorts of mixed signals from myself as I pulled my hair back. Not my type. Too young. I had other things to worry about. Besides, I said no more NASCAR drivers. Not to mention I would have to deal with Finn.

Shit, Finn. Should I text him? No. That could wait until later. *Much* later.

I texted London. My sister was the entire reason I had even come to the track in the first place. London was talented. So fucking talented and I needed to make sure she was able to keep going to Juilliard. She asked questions about Finn and if any of the drivers were cute. I ignore that last part. I wasn't about to drag my baby sister into this mess. After promising to call her tonight, I decided to pack up my shit and head home.

I stopped for breakfast at some little greasy spoon outside of town. I had my favorite breakfast of Belgian waffles with strawberries and whipped cream. The coffee wasn't much to write home about, but I drank it anyway. It made me think of my favorite coffee shop back home and I couldn't wait to get back there tomorrow morning.

After my breakfast, I hit the road again with some Taylor Swift blasting through my speakers. I had seen a sign for a used bookstore on my way to the diner and sure enough, I got lost in there. For what felt like days. It had only been two hours, but when I saw it was two o'clock, I knew I had to get moving. I dumped my new books into my car and headed off to the highway.

Except, my car had other plans for me.

I heard the noise my old beat-up Ford was making and I knew it wasn't good. I had hoped I could make it up to New Hampshire and back again without a problem. I didn't use my car much back home. I knew I needed a new car, but couldn't afford one right now. I smacked my hands against the steering wheel. "Please don't do this to me right now."

I wasn't against begging for things I really needed.

I had to get off this highway before my car blew up on me. "Come on, old girl." I eased my foot off the gas as I turned my right blinker on. "We're going to be alright."

We were *not* going to be alright, but why tell my car that?

I managed to make it to the first rest stop without any problems. I called AAA knowing all my money that I had earned from this weekend was disappearing. I wasn't going to cry about it, even though I wanted to. I was used to getting screwed out of things I needed and this wouldn't be the first time it happened. Or the last.

I settled on the hood of my car with one of my new books and waited for the tow truck.

"Hello, darlin'."

I looked up over the book and when I saw Rand standing in front of me, I nearly fell off the car. "What the fuck are you doing here?"

"I was about to ask you the same question." Rand tilted his head when he looked at me. He was wearing a pair of tight blue jeans that fit him just perfectly and a t-shirt that hugged every single muscle on his chest like a second skin.

I got to my feet. "Don't you have a race to finish?" I glared up at him. I was so glad he had on those damn sunglasses again.

"Don't you have a race to photograph?" he shot back at me. A smirk appeared on Rand's face as we stared at one another. "Do you need a ride?"

"I am waiting on a tow truck," I snapped. "What happened to the race?"

"My engine blew." Rand ran a hand through his thick hair. "Not a good day all around for the team." He looked a bit defeated.

Before I could stop myself, I put my hand on Rand's arm.

"I'm sorry. I know it's hard when you worked hard all week for a great race."

His whole body seemed to change. "It sucks, really. I had a great damn car, too. I was running top five when the engine gave out." Rand chuckled. "Looks like we're both having a shitty car day." He looked down at where my hand was still on his arm and when I went to move it, Rand placed his other hand over mine. "Let me give you a ride home, darlin'." He moved so that he had me pinned against my car.

"Rand—" I suddenly realized that I wanted to be totally destroyed by Rand Shepard. I wanted him to completely ruin me with pleasure until I couldn't stand it. And then? I wanted him to do it again.

"I'll make sure your car gets home, too." Rand's southern accent seemed to get thicker when he was trying to smooth talk me. Was it like that with every woman? "Pop the trunk, let's go."

"You're just going to what? Give me a ride home in your RV? Won't your driver care?" I shook my head and pressed my hand against his chest. "I'm good."

"Who, Jimbo? Nope, he won't care if we make a little detour. Now do I have to take your keys from you?" Rand pulled his sunglasses down so I could see his baby blues. "I'll do it, you know I will." I felt his hand against my thigh. "Which pocket?"

I shivered at his touch. In this weather, I should be sweating, but not when Rand Shepard put his hands on me. "You're warm," I murmured and fought back the urge to moan when his hand slipped into my pocket. I hated myself.

"Was that so hard, darlin'?" Rand pushed his glasses back

up as he went to the back of the car. "Let's get all this shit in the RV and get you out of here." He pulled out my bags. "It's much cooler in there, I promise you."

I was just waiting for the warning bells to go off inside my head again. Where were they? They seemed to have sort of disappeared on me. No bells, no whistles. Just my heart pounding at how close Rand had gotten to me again. And I fucking let him.

"Do I have to carry you, too?" Rand teased me from the side of the RV. "I can do that. If you really want me to."

Hadn't I told the man to stay away from me? Didn't I slap him this morning? Why was he being so nice to me? With a sigh, I started toward the RV. "I'm not sleeping with you again." Those were the first words out of my mouth when I walked inside.

A big wide grin exploded onto Rand's face. "Did I say anything about sex? Why do you have to make everything about sex, Brooklyn?" He put his head back and laughed. It was the first time I had really heard him laugh like that.

"You never call me Sully." I bit down on my bottom lip as I watched him. I was curious about the man. I couldn't deny that.

"Do you want me to call you that?" Rand went over and grabbed two waters, handing me one as the RV started moving. "I like Brooklyn, it's your name." He sat across from me.

"My friends—" Was Rand my friend? "My friends call me Sully." I finished the sentence and took a long drink of water, nearly finishing the entire bottle.

"Is that what we are now, darlin'?" Rand's lips turned up

into a smile again. *"Friends?"*

"What else would we be?" I didn't like where this conversation was going. I didn't like that Rand was standing up and moving to sit next to me. His body heat was overpowering. *He* was overpowering.

"I don't know." Rand turned my face so that I had to look at him. He ran his thumb across my bottom lip as he watched me without saying anything. Then he pulled me onto his lap, his lips fluttering against mine. "What are you doing to me, Brooklyn?"

The way Rand said my name was the only way I wanted it to be said. I only wanted him to say it. "What do you mean?" There was no tongue involved with this kiss. Just soft lips as our eyes stayed locked together.

"I can't think about anyone else," Rand whispered. "Your face is behind my eyes when I close them." He pushed a piece of hair behind my ear. "What are we going to do about this, darlin'?"

I felt his erection pressed against my shorts and I rubbed my pussy against it. Right through my shorts. "You said you didn't date." I licked around Rand's lips with my tongue. "You weren't boyfriend material."

Rand's hands gripped my hips. "I did say that." His tongue snaked inside my mouth this time and swirled around. I loved how it felt rubbing against mine as I ground against his hard cock. "I want you so bad."

I moaned into Rand's mouth. "Rand… I won't… I can't be that girl." His hand slipped up my shirt and found my nipple over my bra. Our kisses became rougher and harder as we dry humped one another.

Rand's lips moved to my ear. "Be my girl, darlin'."

I stopped and stared at him. "What?" I swear he just told me to be his girl.

"I want you to be my girl, Brooklyn." Rand's eyes were wide and he looked serious.

"I—" I climbed off his lap. "I need to—I don't know if— why?" I wasn't sure what was going on right now.

Rand stood up. "Don't say no. Don't say anything yet. Let's spend some time together first. Let me spend a couple days at your place."

"You want to come to my place?" This was insane. I was losing my mind.

"Yes, if that's alright." Rand's eyes looked almost scared. "Please."

He was taking a chance with me. Rand must have been hurt before and now he was taking a chance with me. "Sure, alright. Okay." I nodded my head. "Yes."

Rand pulled me against him tightly. "I promise I won't be a complete asshole." He laughed softly.

<u>Chapter Seven</u>
RAND

My day had turned to shit the moment I walked into the garage. Everyone was giving me the stink eye because of the whole Travis thing and Finn wouldn't talk to me because of Brooklyn.

I get the Travis thing. I went to his party and broke his nose. I actually did, too. Break his nose. I half expected to get arrested for assault, but luckily that didn't happen.

Wouldn't be the first time if it did though.

So, it was only fitting that my car be a flaming pile of shit, too. I knew the moment I got behind the wheel something wasn't right. It just felt off. I knew I had a top ten car, maybe even a winning car. But, not if the engine was going to blow up halfway through the race.

Finn's engine went first. We were about fifty laps into the race.

Mine went two laps later.

Of course, we both had to play nice and talk to the press after. Usually it was fine, the two of us together. We weren't best friends, never would be, but the tension was so tight between us, I just knew that everyone could feel it.

Did I need to remind the man that *he* came to *me* to take Brooklyn to the party?

I thought about it. But I let it go. I had been in Finn's shoes before. The hurting, the embarrassment over the woman—or in my case, girl—you loved choosing someone else. But, if he kept up the shit he was pulling, I would confront him.

I had hung around for a bit after that. Talked to a few fans that were looking for autographs and pictures. I loved my fans. They were the ones that I wanted to win for. Sure, I wanted to win for myself, but if it wasn't for the fans, I wouldn't be here. They bought my merchandise, they came to the races and they were the reason I wanted to be the best NASCAR driver I could be.

I knew I was seriously off my game when I turned down a pit bunny. If you aren't familiar with what a pit bunny is, I'll make it simple for you. It's a woman that comes to the track looking to fuck a driver. She's usually dressed in pretty much nothing and it's clear what she's looking for. I always made sure to never pick the same one twice. However, today, I didn't pick one at all.

I thought maybe I was sick. Or maybe the heat was getting to me. Which would be odd considering I grew up in Georgia and was used to this sort of weather. Or maybe it was the shitty way my day ended. I had a good thing going lately with my races. I was so close to getting my first win, I could taste it.

It wasn't until Jim, my driver, pulled into the rest stop that

I knew what my problem really was. I stepped out of the RV to find Brooklyn sitting there on the back of her car, and I thought I was dreaming. That the lack of sleep, the heat, and lack of food had finally caught up with me.

Except, it hadn't. Brooklyn was really fucking there and I realized that *she* was my problem. Brooklyn had come into my life in just one damn day and gotten under my skin like one of my tattoos.

I wanted her. I wanted her in more ways than one. Sure, I wanted to kiss her and fuck her. That was a given. But I wanted Brooklyn to be mine. *My girl.* This was damn crazy because I didn't date and I didn't have girlfriends.

Right now I was kissing her again. After telling Brooklyn I wanted to go to her house. Fuck, I'd go to the ends of the earth for this woman. I felt her body tremble as the kiss went on, as I let my tongue find hers. She was a good, solid girl. I needed that in my life. I wanted that in my life.

Brooklyn's hands clung to the back of my t-shirt as I tried to kiss away her doubts and fears. I cradled her head in my hands as I tasted her sweetness, until I knew she was breathless and I had to pull away.

"Rand." My name on Brooklyn's lips was the most arousing thing I had ever heard. Her plump lips were swollen from kissing and I had to stop myself from going back for more. Her dark eyes moved over my face as she took a step back.

"Don't be shy now, darlin'." I reached for her hand. "We both know how this is going to go down."

"I—" Brooklyn's eyes grew round and I saw the look of lust

followed by fear.

Shit, okay. Before we fucked again, I had to assure her I wasn't going to hurt her. I could do that. I would have to open up some of my own wounds. Some secrets that I had been hiding for a while or maybe that I had never shared. There were some deep ones that I had hidden away. I ran my hand down the front of my face and took a deep breath.

"Rules, you wanted to set some." I smiled down into her beautiful face. "Let's talk then." I would have a serious case of blue balls, but my cock would have to rest for now. I sat back down and patted the cushion next to me. "Come on now, darlin'."

Brooklyn sat down and I pulled her into my lap, causing her to let out a little laugh. I needed her near me... no, fuck that. I needed her so close to me that I could touch her. "Jesus, Rand." She touched my face. "I'm right here. Can't I sit on my own?" She giggled softly. "I like sitting on you. You're big." Her face immediately turned red.

"Thank you." I chuckled and my heart felt funny. Like twisted and jumpy.

"I didn't mean it like that, perv." Brooklyn rested her head on my shoulder. "I meant that you're just so much larger than I am. I'm hardly even five two and you're just this big, tree trunk of a man. I could just climb you like—" She snorted and buried her face in my neck. "I'm not helping things at all." Brooklyn's lips brushed against my skin, making my cock strain against my jeans.

Down, boy. "You're not," I teased her. "I like how small you are. Like this little petite flower that I can carry around in my pocket." I waited for her reaction.

"Excuse me?" Brooklyn was in my face. "In your pocket?"

"Gotcha." I wanted to kiss her again. I wanted to bury my face between her legs and make her come. I wanted to make Brooklyn scream my name over and over again. I wanted her pussy wrapped around my cock. I wanted her lips wrapped around my cock.

I wanted her. I only wanted her. What the fuck?

Brooklyn touched my lips with her fingers lightly. Pressing the pads against my top lip, gliding them across softly before moving down to the bottom and doing the same. "Talk to me, Rand. I need to know you're not going to break my heart. Promise me you won't do that."

I would rather die than hurt Brooklyn. The thought was so loud in my head that it scared me. "I won't hurt you, darlin'," I assured her and nipped at her fingers.

"Promise me." Brooklyn sounded sad. "It's not just the other women or the—"

"It's the cars, too. I know the risks." I had been a driver long enough to understand what could happen. My parents hadn't wanted me to be a driver. They had fought it so hard and so long that when I finally made it, I cut them out of my life.

I grew up poor. With no help from them. I did everything on my own and now they wanted to be a part of my life? I think the fuck not.

"I know you can't promise me that you won't get hurt, Rand." Brooklyn moved slightly on my lap. "I know that. Just assure me that you'll do your best to be safe. To drive safely, to be safe around the others and—to not hurt me." Her hand touched my cheek.

"I promise to never hurt you." I took her hand and pressed it to my lips. "I promise to drive as safe as I can. I promise to make sure to drive safe around the other drivers." I kissed her hand again. "Brooklyn, your heart is safe with me."

"Rules, Rand," she said again. "We need to make them. I don't want you to say one thing now and then next weekend end up fucking some pit bunny. If you do that, it's over. I won't be made a fool."

"Of course." I realized then that she wasn't just talking about me. Cooper Houston might have been her first love, but he might have also hurt her, too. "I won't make a fool of you, darlin'."

"I won't hurt you either, Rand," Brooklyn said softly. "So, I'm your girl? And, you're my boy?" She smiled.

"I guess that sounds about right." I dipped her onto the couch. "Although, I prefer man." I pinned her against the cushions. "Now kiss me again, darlin'." I pressed my lips against hers and felt everything from the day start to melt away.

"Rand." There it was again, my name on her lips. I wanted to record the sound of Brooklyn saying just my name so I could listen to it when she wasn't around. Her hand came up to touch my cheek. Clearly this wasn't going to go the way I wanted. I would be fine with a fifteen-minute make-out session, but Brooklyn had other ideas.

"Tell me what made you like this." Her brown eyes

searched my blues.

Her question caught me off guard and I raised my eyebrow at her. "Like what?" I leaned down to kiss her again. "You're serious? What do you mean 'like this'? Brooklyn, I'm me." I helped her up into a sitting position again. "I've always been like this. Well, the tattoos I added, but—"

"Tell me the truth." Brooklyn stopped me. "Who was she?"

I didn't want to go back to that time in my life. I hated it. I was a young, stupid kid who thought he was in love and I felt a wave of hate spill from me. "Darlin', I don't want her here," I finally answered.

"Cooper cheated on me." Brooklyn's voice was barely a whisper when she spoke. "We were so young when we met and I guess, maybe, he wanted to explore his options." She wasn't looking at me anymore. Instead, she was staring down at her hands. "I loved him so much. I was twelve when I met Cooper and I was smitten. I thought he was, too, but looking back on it, he wasn't crazy in love with me. Not like I was with him." She sniffed softly. "I should have broken up with him, but I was afraid to be alone. Afraid that I would never find someone that would like me."

The cruel flower of anger started to bloom inside me as I listened to Brooklyn. I had never met Cooper Houston and right now I was glad for that. How could he treat someone like Brooklyn like that? She was so damn perfect. I reached for her hands, but she pulled them away from me. "Her name was Nora Heron. Is that what you wanted to hear?" I jumped up off the couch. "You want to compare war stories, darlin'? See who has the worst one?"

Brooklyn shook her head. "Don't try to pick a fight with me, Rand." She stared up at me. "I want you to talk to me."

Fuck. FUCK! I didn't want to do this. I hated that bitch and what she did to me. Her friends, too. I became this version of me because of her. Nora was a— I turned around and there was Brooklyn. Waiting for me to continue my story. I shook my head. "Please, please I don't want to go back to that place."

Brooklyn patted the seat next to her and I started toward her, but instead, I ended up on my knees, my head in her lap.

Call me whatever you want, this woman was what I fucking needed.

Brooklyn ran her hands through my hair while I talked. While I told her everything that happened with Nora. About how when I was thirteen years old, I had a huge crush on her. She was the most popular girl in school and I thought she was so amazing. Just like most of the other guys.

"I finally got the nerve to ask Nora out." I gritted my teeth as the memory seared through my brain. "The bitch actually said yes. I was so excited. So, of course, neither one of us was old enough to drive, so she asked me to come over to watch a movie. Said her parents weren't going to be home." I hated how weak this made me sound. Brooklyn's fingers continued to weave through my hair.

"I was thirteen. *Thirteen.* I didn't know a fucking thing about sex. I didn't have an older brother to tell me about it and my parents never told me shit." I sat back on my knees thinking about how I would probably have to tell her about Eli sooner or later, but later would be better. "I lasted about three seconds. Nora told everyone in school about it. All her cheerleader friends. All the football guys. But, of course, she let me think everything was fine when I went home that night. It wasn't until I got to school on Monday morning that I realized it wasn't." I realized that the RV had stopped. "We must be close to your place." I stood up. "That your house?"

Brooklyn nodded. "Yes." She smiled at me and reached for my hand. "Rand—"

I knew she had more questions about Nora. I wasn't ready to go any farther down that rabbit hole right now. Instead, I grabbed her, flipping her over my shoulder. The sound of Brooklyn's laughter was music to my ears and it pushed Nora and everything else back to where they belonged.

Chapter Eight
SULLY

I was laughing so hard at the fact that Rand literally threw me over his shoulder and carried me toward my house. He placed me on my feet once we reached the front door and I could only imagine what my neighbors were thinking right about now.

"I'll go get our bags, darlin'. Be back in a minute." Rand winked at me and off he went again. Sprinting down my front lawn like he did it all the time. Like he belonged here.

Wait. *What?*

Back up, Sully. Yes, there was some serious chemistry between the two of us, there was no denying that. But I didn't *know* him. The story Rand told me earlier was horrible and I didn't even hear the entire thing. It was like pulling teeth to get him to even tell me what had happened.

I realized I had been standing at my front door with my keys clutched to my chest and turned to open the door. I had splurged last fall and purchased central air and the coolness that hit me when I walked into the foyer was wonderful. I kept the door open so Rand could come inside and I headed upstairs.

It was going to be strange having another man in the house and I hope that Rand didn't feel awkward with memories of Cooper around. We had bought this home together, although he had spent a lot of time in North Carolina with his team. Before the crash.

There were only three parts of my life.

Life with Cooper. The crash. Now.

"Darlin', where are you?" Rand called to me from below.

A faint smile pulled at my lips when I heard Rand call to me, and I came back to meet him at the top of the stairs. "Everything all set?" I asked him.

Rand ran his hand through his dark hair and I saw the sweat that had broken out on his face. "Perfect." He ran up the stairs two at a time. "Where should I put these?" He motioned to the two bags he held in his hands.

I jutted my chin toward the hall. "This way." Were we sharing a bed? I assumed that was part of the deal. "This is—" I shared this bed with Cooper. I still had his things here. I looked up as Rand looked around.

"Do you want me to sleep in here with you?" Rand had put the bags on the floor. "I can sleep somewhere else if that will make you feel better." His eyes flicked toward the room across the hallway.

I grabbed his arm. "I want you in my bed."

Rand nodded and then pulled me against him. He didn't say anything as his lips met mine, his tongue slipping inside my mouth. God, the man knew how to kiss and I felt a wild surge of electricity starting to build inside me. Rand's tongue was savage as it rolled around inside my mouth, fighting for control against my own.

"Rand," I panted when I pulled back, my chest heaving up and down.

Rand growled deep inside his chest. "Do you know what it does to me when you say my name?" I could feel how aroused he was. "It drives me fucking insane." He pushed me back until I could feel the bed against my legs. "I want you, darlin'. I want you so bad." His hands were already pulling at my shorts.

I felt the heat that had been building in my belly start to coil through the rest of my body. "Fuck me, Rand." I was shocked at the words that came out of my mouth, but everything about me seemed to change around this man. I helped him with my shorts and then went for his jeans.

"Look at you," Rand teased me. "So eager right now." He let me pull down his zipper. "Now what, darlin'?" He tucked a finger under my chin. "Want me to take them off?"

I nodded as a shiver of desire shot through my body. I watched as Rand removed his jeans and his beautiful, hard cock popped out at me. I also loved how he didn't bother to wear underwear. "Jesus, your dick is gorgeous." I knew Rand had to know that already and I'm sure I wasn't the first girl to tell him that.

"I'm glad you like it." Rand reached down and wrapped his hand around the shaft. "How about you get those panties off. That top and bra, too, before I die from not being inside you."

I slowly pulled my shirt up over my head before dropping it

on the floor. I did the same with my bra. My nipples were already hard, but when the cool air hit them, they pebbled and tightened even more. I had always hated how small my boobs were, but by the way Rand was looking at me right now, he seemed to appreciate them. I wiggled out of my underwear last.

"You still have your shirt on." I wanted to touch his chest. His arms. Everything. I wanted Rand's naked body against mine. "If I'm naked, you have to be."

Rand never lost eye contact with me as he removed his shirt. "I'm going to fuck you now. I'm going to make you come so hard that your neighbors hear you." His arm snaked around my waist as he pulled me against him again. "Then I'm going to do it again." His lips brushed my lips.

"Yes." I moaned at his dirty talk and when Rand lifted me up, I instinctively wrapped my legs around his waist like we'd done this a million times before. I could already feel the head of his swollen cock at my entrance and I arched my hips toward him trying to urge him inside.

Rand thrust inside me without a word and I cried out, digging my nails into his back. Just like the first time, I was already spiraling toward climax the moment he was inside me. Rand's dick had been inside me for about thirty seconds and I was going to come.

His cock seemed to hit all the right spots and I wanted to tell him to stop. I wasn't ready for it to be over; Rand had hardly even touched me. A raw rippling wave began to wash over me and I heard myself scream Rand's name as he pressed me down against the mattress. He pressed harder into me. My body was tingling all over as I started to come down from my orgasm and I already felt another one building in my spine.

"Fuck," Rand whispered. "Watching you come was so hot." His lips brushed mine. "You think you can do that again?" He bucked his hips up against mine and he leaned down to take one of my nipples into his mouth.

I arched toward him, the extra contact making me writhe underneath him. My entire body felt like it was on fire and I gripped Rand's shoulders. A blissful, blistering pleasure seized me and it was like nothing I had ever felt before. I heard myself screaming for Rand to fuck me.

Harder. Faster. More.

Rand's breath was coming out in jagged gasps and I could tell he was getting closer. His back was covered in beads of perspiration and sweat dripped from his brow. "Darlin'—" He came with a loud cry and I felt his cock jerking inside me as I came again with him, my bones turning to liquid as we both surrendered to one another.

Rand fell onto the bed next to me trying to catch his breath and I turned onto my side to watch him. He had his arm over his eyes and he pulled it down slowly to look at me, a sly smile spreading across his beautiful face. "You continue to surprise me, darlin'." His accent sounded thicker and I resisted the urge to climb on top of him again.

"Are you hungry?" I asked softly. "We can order a piz—"

Rand stopped me with a kiss, his hands slipping down my sides and tracing the contours of my body. "Pizza sounds wonderful," he whispered when he pulled away. "Anything but anchovies, because they are the devil."

I stood up, grabbing my underwear off the floor. "There's a great little place down the street we can order from." I turned to see Rand watching me, his arms behind his head. Jesus Christ. He was so fucking gorgeous I could hardly breathe when I looked at him. "I'll go put the order in."

Fuck. Me. I was in trouble.

***

Rand and I devoured a large pizza. Or should I say, Rand did. He claimed he was a growing boy and needed his food. I remembered the days when Cooper would come home exhausted and dehydrated from a race. I knew what it could do to a person if they didn't take care of themselves.

We had settled into the downstairs family room. A place I didn't spend a lot of time in these days. London had a room down here, which is one of the reasons why I had wanted this house in the first place. It had the extra room built off the back of the house and it was perfect for my sister. She kept her piano in the back corner, along with some of her music, so I always thought of it as her place. Even though my studio was where the garage used to be.

"You play?" Rand gestured toward the piano after wiping his hands with a napkin. There was a movie on the big screen television but neither one of us seemed to be watching it. I was too distracted by Rand and the fact that he was only wearing a pair of boxer shorts. Rand's eyes moved around the room looking at everything, like he was just soaking it all in.

I giggled. "Me? Oh, fuck no." I wrinkled my nose at the

thought. "It's my sister's. She's at college now."

"Your sister lives with you?" Rand tilted his head. "What about your parents?"

"My parents..." I sighed. "I don't talk to my parents. My grandparents raised me and London. They retired to Florida a few years ago. They come back for Thanksgiving and stay until New Year's." *Please don't ask me about my shitty parents*, I silently begged him. I'd tell him if he asked. I'd probably give him my ATM pin number if he asked me.

What. The Fuck.

Rand stood up and walked over to the piano. "May I?"

I waved my hand toward the instrument. "Please."

Rand sat down and started playing. He was amazing, which honestly didn't surprise me. I wasn't sure what the song was, but it was beautiful and I found myself moving closer to him as I watched Rand's fingers glide across the keys. Was there anything the man couldn't do? When he was done, Rand smiled up at me. "I'm a little rusty, but I think I still remembered some of it." His smile grew into a big toothy grin and I swear my heart nearly stopped.

"Rand, that was amazing." I clapped my hands together.

"Eight years of classes, thank you very much." He chuckled. "Can I see your studio?" He was already on his feet again, holding out his hand.

I led him down the hall and flipped the lights on, watching as Rand moved around. I loved my studio. I loved my job. I was heading down a bad road, even with Cooper in my life, until I discovered I was good at taking pictures. I was around sixteen when that happened.

"These are good, darlin'." Rand was looking at one of the pictures I had up of Finn and Cooper. Shit. "You really have an eye for this."

"I'll get the ones I took this weekend developed tomorrow. I want to see how the ones I took of you came out." I wrapped my arms around his back. "I need to update my pictures."

Rand stiffened. "Don't do that." He pulled my arms away from him and turned around, his blue eyes blazing. "Don't change things because of me."

"Rand, I didn't—" I was confused. "I thought…"

"Thought what?" Rand grunted. "I don't need you to put my picture on the wall to prove something, Brooklyn." He sounded angry now.

"I didn't say that. I want to put your picture up. You're my guy, right?" I felt my stomach twist and my pizza threatened to come back up.

"Sure, right." Rand nodded. "You know, I need to call my PR girl. She's probably a little pissed at me since I blew off a couple of things. Think I'll make the call outside."

I was going to fucking explode on him. Rand was the one that told me he wanted me to be his girl. That he wanted me. I didn't come to him. Well, the first night, sure. I bit back tears as I heard the back door open and slide shut again. I could see him in the dark as the floodlights were triggered and Rand made his way over to the pool, his cell phone up to his ear.

Bastard.

I decided now would be a good time to call London, since I

was overdue.

"Hey, Sis!" London's cheerful voice instantly warmed my heart when she picked up. "How was New Hampshire?" I could hear talking in the background and I wondered if I was disturbing her.

"I shouldn't have gone, but the money will be worth it." I sat down on the couch and muted the television. "How's school?

London sounded muffled for a second and I realized she had her hand over the speaker. My sister was no longer a kid. At eighteen, she was now legally an adult and probably trying to hide things from me. "Sorry, Sully. I was—" She giggled. "Can I call you back?"

I smiled. I wanted my sister to be happy. "Don't call me back, Lon. Just have fun and practice safe sex," I teased her.

"OMG!" London laughed. "I love you. I'll text you."

Rand was still outside on his phone and from the looks of things, he looked upset. His hand was up in the air and he shook his head. I didn't want to deal with that. I was still upset about how he treated me earlier and I decided to go to bed. He could either join me later or sleep somewhere else.

I wasn't sure what time Rand finally came to bed, but I felt the mattress dip down when he slipped in next to me. He wrapped his arms around me and pulled me close, his face in my hair. I pretended to be asleep, but I'm pretty sure he knew I wasn't.

"I'm your guy, darlin'," Rand whispered softly.

I fell asleep not too long after that.

Chapter Nine
SULLY

When I woke up the next morning, Rand was wrapped around me like a bad rash and even though I was still upset about what happened last night, I took a few minutes to enjoy his peaceful expression. I brushed the dark hair back from Rand's forehead, hoping that I didn't wake him.

I knew that whatever happened with Nora had hardened him. It must have been so devastating that Rand hadn't mentioned it to his parents, but he did mention he was an only child. Didn't he have some friends that he could go to at least if his parents weren't there? What kind of a girl would do that to a boy anyway?

My blood boiled at the words Rand had told me. He hadn't told me the complete story—I needed to push him for more—but I got the gist of it. Kids can be cruel and girls were the worst.

My heart felt strange around Rand Shepard. Not like when I was with Cooper. Cooper was someone that I knew for so long and thought was the one. Even after everything he had done to me, I knew he would settle down and marry me. He had put a ring on my finger and I would have married him, too. Despite how Cooper had hurt me.

Rand groaned softly and I felt his grip loosen from me. He shifted slightly in the bed and moved onto his back. I felt... disappointed? I knew that he was sleeping and I had things to do today, but I had enjoyed Rand holding me like that.

I touched Rand's face lightly with just the pads of my fingers before I climbed off the bed. I had pictures to look at, a client coming to the studio at eleven and I should probably check in with Finn. The first thing I really wanted to do was get in a run before it got too hot. I didn't like to go more than a day or two without one and it felt like a week since I had laced up my sneakers.

I dug around for my running clothes and slipped out of the bedroom to go change. I knew I should let Rand know where I was in case he woke up while I was out and thought about texting him. That's when I realized I didn't even have his number. I pulled my hair back into a ponytail and flipped the bathroom light off before heading into the kitchen. My pack of sticky notes was sitting on the counter and I jotted down a quick note that I stuck on the bathroom mirror. Then I grabbed my cell phone, put on my running sneakers, and headed out the front door.

The sun was coming up as I hit the asphalt and I headed down my usual route. I always made sure to stick to well-traveled roads where there were cars and people. There were other runners, walkers and bike riders out, which didn't surprise me. Most people would want to get their workouts in before it got too hot, but I just enjoyed getting my run in early. I felt like I could conquer the world when I got in a good three to five miles.

On my way back, I stopped at my favorite coffee shop and grabbed two coffees.

I wasn't sure how Rand liked his coffee, but I hoped the gesture would be appreciated. I also couldn't resist the two chunky looking cheese Danishes I saw sitting behind the glass case either. So, I took those back with me, too.

The house was still quiet when I got back. I popped my head into my bedroom to find Rand spread out still sleeping. He had his mouth wide open and I swore I could hear a little bit of snoring coming from him.

I knew I was still upset about last night, but I also knew that he must have felt bad about it when he came to bed last night. Why else would Rand have told me he was mine?

My stomach felt all bubbly and strange when I thought about that. Again, nothing like when I was with Cooper. I had to stop *that*, too. Comparing this—whatever it was—to what I had with Cooper.

I jumped in the shower to rinse off all the sweat from my run. I also pulled the sticky note off and tossed that into the garbage. I was home now, so Rand could find me if he needed me. I stood under the water for what felt like forever and when I finally climbed out of the tub, I stared at myself in the mirror.

"What are you doing, Sully?" I whispered to myself. "He's eight years younger than you." I chewed on my lip while I pulled my unruly wet hair back into a bun. I sighed and slapped some lotion onto my skin before grabbing my dirty clothes off the floor.

Once I changed into fresh clothes, I headed downstairs to start my day with coffee and Danish in hand. I felt a little more like myself, despite the fact that I had a man sleeping in my bed. I started working on my photos from the race and before long I realized that it was nearly ten o'clock.

My eyes moved to the picture on the wall, the one that had set Rand off last night. It had been two years. I could remove it and replace it with something else, just maybe not with NASCAR. Maybe with a wedding or newborn. I'd have to find a good one.

"Morning, darlin'." Rand's soft voice caught me off guard. He was leaning against the doorway in a pair of blue jeans and a dark shirt. I noticed how his hair was damp and wondered how long he had been awake.

I blushed when I met his eyes. "Good morning." I moved my glasses from my face to the desk. "Sleep okay?" I pointed toward the extra coffee and bakery bag. "I got these for you. I didn't know how you took your coffee, but there's sugar and cream over by the coffeemaker if you need them." I gestured toward the machine I kept downstairs.

Rand's eyes lit up. "You got me coffee?" He looked happy as a pig in shit. He pushed off from the door frame to make his way closer.

"I stopped at my favorite coffee place after my run this morning. Thought you might like—" I stopped when Rand dropped to his knees in front of me. "What are you doing?"

"I'm so sorry, darlin'." Rand's eyes were pleading with me.

Nearly *begging* me, it seemed. "About last night... about what happened and what I said. I'm just... I'm not used to this whole boyfriend-girlfriend thing."

"Rand, it's alright." I didn't like the look in his eyes. It hurt me.

He shook his head. "It's not." Rand took my hands in his. "You are this wondrous light and I keep trying to stomp it out. You deserve so much more."

Fuck Nora Heron. I would punch her in the face if I ever met her. I *swear* to God. "Baby—" The word slipped out of my mouth before I could stop it. "Rand," I corrected myself. "You are a good man. I wish you would give yourself more credit."

His blue eyes moved over my face. "I liked that." A smile pulled at his pink lips. "Call me baby, Brooklyn." Rand moved closer to me and let his head fall into my lap.

I tunneled my hands through his dark hair, feeling the moisture against my skin. "Baby." My voice was so soft I wasn't sure he heard me. So instead, I changed the subject. "Tell me about one of your tattoos," I teased him.

Rand chuckled. "Which one?" He kept his head pressed against my legs.

I knew nothing about tattoos. "The first one." I decided after a few seconds.

"I was hardly old enough to get it." Rand ran his fingers against my calf. "I knew a guy who did it without caring that I was underage." Shit, I kept forgetting he was eight years younger than I was. Sure, Rand acted his age, but his eyes said so much more. I had to talk to him about that. Did he know I was twenty-eight, and did it bother him?

He sat back on his knees to look at me. "I wanted something that would describe me. Who I felt I was. But, I also wanted to make sure the kids in school saw it, too."

"The phoenix." I reached out and touched Rand's neck. "You made a big statement." It was a colorful tattoo with a lot of red and orange as well as some purple thrown in. "I like it."

Rand grabbed my hand. "Brooklyn—"

"Am I interrupting?" My best friend Harper Rose burst into my studio, her auburn hair blazing behind her. Her grey eyes landed on me and moved to where Rand was. "Well, it sure looks like I am." She raised her eyebrows.

Rand jumped to his feet, but stayed next to me.

"Harper." I sighed. I had been avoiding her texts and calls since about eight this morning. I knew Finn must have already contacted her or else she wouldn't be here. "I've been busy, I'm sorry I didn't get back to you."

Harper narrowed her eyes. "Clearly. What's going on here, Sully?" She crossed her arms across her chest.

Rand took a step toward her. "Rand Shepard." He stuck out his hand.

For a minute I thought Harper was going to ignore him, but instead she took his hand. "I know who you are, Shepard. Why do you think I'm here?"

"Oh." Rand turned to look at me. "Should I... do you want me to... you know what? I'll just go."

"That's a good idea. I need to talk to my best friend." Harper sounded different. Not like her usual self.

What. *The.* Fuck?

"Rand." I touched his arm.

"It's alright, darlin'." Rand flashed a smile at me. "I don't want to come between friends. I'll go check on your car." He leaned down and brushed his lips against my cheek. Then he turned to look over his shoulder. "Nice meeting you, Harper."

Once Rand was out of the room, I turned my gaze on my best friend.

"What's the problem, Harp?" I shook my head. "You're not usually so hostile."

"Rand Shepard, Sully?" Harper hissed. "Do you have any idea *who* he is? Why is he at your house right now?"

I pointed toward one of my empty chairs. "Let's talk."

"I don't want to sit down." Harper shook her head. "I want to know what's going on. I've been trying to get ahold of you all morning. Finn is worried—"

My eyebrows shot up. "Finn isn't my dad. I wish he'd butt the fuck out of my life sometimes." I let out a small sigh. "Look, I know he means well, but I'm a big girl, Harp. Trust me; I didn't expect to bring Rand home with me. Can't you just be happy for me? Isn't that what both of you want? You've been telling me that after all this time I should get out and meet someone. What happened to stop sitting around and moping?"

Harper slumped into the chair I had suggested a few minutes earlier, just looking at me. I had known her since we were kids and I could see her struggling with her answer. "Sully, there are so many other men out there. Rand isn't known for being a one-woman guy. Sure, he's good looking, but don't you want someone that's going to be there for you? Someone that wants to settle down and start a family?"

"Jesus! Can't I just have a fling first? Who said anything about a family?" I didn't want to have this conversation right now. This was between me and Rand. "What? Why are you looking at me like that?" Harper had a strange look on her face.

"You're in love with him."

What? "Are you insane? What would make you think that?" I exclaimed, but the thought had already been put into my head.

"If he hurts you—" Harper closed her eyes. "You know, Sully." Her eyes flew open again. "Finn loves you."

"I know that," I snapped at her.

"No, Finn *loves* you. He's been in love with you as long as I've known him." Harper's hand moved to touch my arm. "Please be careful. Just promise me that. *Promise* me that. I'm here for you if you need anything."

I heard the car pull up outside which meant my client was here to go over proofs. There was so much to think about right now. I met Harper's gray eyes as we both stood up. "I promise." My voice sounded so strange.

Harper hugged me before pulling back so we could see eye to eye. "I'm your best friend, I won't judge you," she added.

I nodded. "Thank you."

She was gone as quickly as she came and my clients came in looking tan and cheerful from their honeymoon. I had photographed their wedding three weeks ago and they looked just as happy as the last time I saw them. My mind was spinning as I started to go over their proofs with them.

Watching how they acted together.

I just met Rand. I couldn't be in love with him. Right?

Chapter Ten
RAND

I was fucking fucked.

I was a fucking idiot. I hadn't meant to react to Brooklyn like I had. I just got so jealous when I saw those pictures of Cooper and Finn on her wall. I had no right to be jealous. I wasn't a part of her life until just the other day.

When Brooklyn told me she wanted to put my picture on the wall I panicked. It wasn't that I didn't want her to do that, because I did. If Brooklyn wanted to show everyone that I was her boyfriend, then so fucking be it. This is her damn house. She could do whatever the hell she wanted.

I fucking freaked the hell out. I promised Brooklyn that I wouldn't hurt her and what did I do? Get angry. Get mad and walk the fuck out like a fucking ASSHOLE! The thing I told her I wouldn't do.

It was in my blood. It was who I was.

When I came back into her house and found Brooklyn sleeping, I almost left. I had hoped she would be awake and waiting for me. But why should she? I was the fool, not her. I thought about calling an Uber and going to the airport. Leaving Brooklyn was probably the best thing I could do.

Brooklyn deserved someone good. I was hardly the poster boy for that shit.

Yet, I crawled into her warm bed, pulled her close and promised her I was hers.

Like I said, I was fucking *fucked*.

I could only imagine what her friend Harper was telling her now. What horrible and terrible things she would fill Brooklyn's beautiful mind with. I deserved it. I wasn't a good man. I had tried to be, but I just—

I was sitting on the front steps when the car pulled up and parked in the side driveway. I watched as the couple climbed out smiling and laughing with one another. They looked happy. They looked in love. I wondered what it would be like to have that kind of relationship.

The way the woman looked at the man. The way the man looked at the woman.

Would Brooklyn ever want that with me? Would she want to spend the rest of her life with me?

Whoa. I needed to slow my damn roll for a second. I had just met Brooklyn, why was I thinking about shit like that? Jesus Christ. What was going on in my damn head? I needed to think. No, that was my problem. I kept thinking about stupid shit like this. Shit that didn't make sense.

I stood up and moved from the concrete steps, toward the side of the house, away from Brooklyn's studio. I needed to call about her car anyway, find out what was going on with it. I had a feeling that the thing was toast. I had noticed it had a lot of miles on it when we had gone to the party on Saturday night, so I was assuming the worst.

I pulled my phone from my pocket and dialed my buddy Ethan.

"Shepard! Long time no see, my man." Ethan's raspy voice boomed loudly in my ear. I could hear the sounds of the garage in the background making me a little homesick.

"Ethan, I'm hoping you have an update on that blue Ford for me." I turned at the sound of beeping behind me and was surprised to see it was Harper. She gave me a small wave as she started her car. Was I just transported into an alternate dimension? I waved back and shook my head.

Fucking odd.

"The one from Connecticut, right?" Ethan grumbled. He wasn't angry; it was just how he was. "I'm afraid it's dead, dude. It's gone on to the car afterlife."

"Shit." I knew Brooklyn couldn't afford a new car.

"Look, I can try to replace the engine—"

"No, man, do you have anything you can sell me? Something similar or close to it?" I started walking down the driveway a bit. Jesus, it was already blazing hot out here.

"I probably have something. Hey, this isn't fucking happy hour, you assholes. Stop bullshitting and get back to work!" Ethan suddenly hollered into my ear. Christ, I did *not* miss any of that nonsense at all. Ethan was a good guy, but when you fucked around on his time-fucking forget it.

I stopped about halfway down Brooklyn's street. "Thanks, man. Send me a picture of what you find. I'll take care of the cost."

Ethan coughed. "Shepard, are you alright?"

"Of course." *What?*

"This girl... she... someone finally got to you," Ethan commented.

"Just text me." I hit the end button on my phone. Jesus, did everyone have something to say about this relationship? I never said shit when Ethan dated Lara. Or when he married Heather. Why does everyone care so much about my love life?

Can't I just fall in love without people sticking their nose into it?

Wait. Was this love? Fuck.

"Um, excuse me?"

I whirled around at the soft voice behind me. Standing there was a blonde-haired woman with dark-green eyes. She was also very, *very* pregnant. "Help you?" I didn't want to be mean since this wasn't my neighborhood, but seriously. Fuck off.

The blonde smiled at me and I noticed how pretty she was, though not really my type. Her hair was pulled back into a frizzy, messy ponytail. Her eyes were a deep emerald color and she had freckles sprinkled across her cheeks. "Sorry, I don't mean to intrude. I'm Mia Knight. I live across the street from Brooklyn." She ran her hand over her protruding stomach. "I was wondering if she was home. I didn't see her car, but I saw you sitting outside so...?" She smiled up at me.

"Oh… uh. Brooklyn's home." I should introduce myself. *Right*? Do I say boyfriend? Or friend? Or— "I'm Rand. Rand Shepard." I plastered on a smile that I hoped didn't look too fake. "She has a client right now, but I'm sure when she's done, she'd love to see you."

What?

"Could you just let her know I was looking for her? It's no big deal. Just, you know, girl stuff." Mia blushed a deep pink.

"Sure, of course." I nodded at her.

This day kept getting weirder and weirder.

I was alone again, so I made my way back to Brooklyn's house. I saw she still had her clients, so I went upstairs to the kitchen. I was starving and had left the Danish she bought me on her desk downstairs. I wondered if she would mind if I made myself something to eat. Or would she be hungry, too? Should I cook for both of us?

I started digging around in Brooklyn's fridge. She didn't have a lot of food, but I found a few things I could work with to make a casserole. I found some bowls in the cabinet and a dish to bake it in and started mixing it together. Then I popped it into the oven at three-seventy-five for thirty minutes before I cleaned up my mess.

"Are you cooking?" Brooklyn giggled softly.

I glanced over my shoulder from the sink. "I am, darlin'. I hope you don't mind." I rinsed off the last utensil before putting it in the dish drainer.

"Are you kidding?" She moved to wrap her arms around me, her head against my chest. "It smells amazing."

I smiled and pulled her closer. "I met your neighbor." Brooklyn looked up at me. "Mia? Very pregnant? She wanted me to tell you she was looking for you."

"Her husband is in the Army and won't be back in time for the birth of her boys. She asked me to be there for her, you know, when they arrive. Mia is super nervous about the whole thing. They were trying to have a baby *forever*. Then poof, she's having twins."

Could this woman be any fucking nicer? "That's real sweet of you, darlin'." I twisted a loose piece of Brooklyn's hair between my fingers. My phone went off, letting me know I had a text message.

"You need to check that?" Brooklyn untangled herself from me.

I shrugged. "Probably, but whatever."

"Rand—"

"I know, darlin'." I nodded. "No secrets, no lies, I know." I pulled my phone out of my pocket. Ethan had sent me a picture of a car along with the price. I held it out to her. "What do you think of this car?"

Brooklyn shrugged. "It's alright. Why? You need a new car?"

"Because it's your next car. Your other one is dead." I texted a quick reply to Ethan to let him know I wanted it.

"I can't afford a new car." Brooklyn's eyes went wide.

"Don't worry about it," I assured her.

"No."

I stared at her. "What?"

"No, Rand. I can't let you buy me a car." Brooklyn looked angry. Why?

"I want to." I moved to pull her back into my arms, but she took a step back. "Brooklyn—"

Brooklyn shook her head. "Absolutely fucking not, Rand Shepard. I'm not a charity case." She crossed her arms over her chest.

Jesus Christ. "I didn't say you were." Was she seriously mad right now?

"I don't want it. Text whoever that is and tell them no." Brooklyn's eyes were narrow as she looked up at me.

But fuck if it didn't make my cock hard. I liked that she wasn't afraid to push me, talk back or tell me no.

"Darlin'." I ran my hand through my hair. "Alright, you win." I shook my head. When I looked at her again, Brooklyn had a faint smile on her face. "What?"

"It was sweet though. You trying to buy me a car." Her voice was full of heat and something else when she spoke. "How long until the food is done?" Brooklyn's eyes moved up my body to my face but I saw the way it lingered on the bulge in my pants.

"Come here, darlin'." I used my index finger to indicate she should move closer. "Or do you want me to come over there?" I watched as Brooklyn ran her tongue across her bottom lip. "Is that a dare?" She tried to move fast, but my legs were longer and I pinned her against the wall in the hallway.

"Rand." Brooklyn trembled against my chest as she met my eyes.

"Tell me what you want, darlin'." I ran my finger across her jaw. I loved how shy Brooklyn got when it came to sex. But now was not the time. "Don't be bashful." I nearly growled at her.

Brooklyn's hand came down to cup my crotch and I swear I nearly exploded in my pants when she dropped to her knees. "Please?"

Who was I to deny a girl?

Chapter Eleven
SULLY

Was I going to give Rand a blowjob in my hallway? Yes, yes I was. Why? Because I fucking wanted to. I had enjoyed sex before, but there was something about Rand that really brought out the beast in me. I looked up at him under my eyelashes and the way his blue eyes hit me, I nearly yanked the zipper right off of his jeans.

"Easy now, darlin'," Rand teased me softly. "My cock isn't going anywhere." He placed his hand lightly on the back of my head.

I didn't say anything to him. I was anxious to taste him, anxious to take him into my mouth. I slipped my hand into Rand's jeans so I could get his penis free. I loved that he was already rock hard and ready for me. I let my fingers close around the hard flesh and Rand let out a low groan, his hand digging into my hair. Then I took his hot cock into my mouth.

"Fuck," Rand grunted deep in his chest. I tried to force my throat to open wider so I could take him deeper just so I could make him feel even better. Not that I didn't enjoy the noises he was making now. "That's good, darlin'. Fuck... uh." Rand's fingers knotted in my hair before slowly pulling his tautness out of my mouth. Then sliding it right back in.

My underwear was instantly wet as I kept my eyes glued to Rand. I loved watching his reaction as I gave him head. I loved the feel of his hands in my hair and how he pulled on it. Not too hard, but just enough to make *my* body come alive.

"You're gonna make me come, darlin'," Rand warned me. "Not that I don't want to, but I'm just giving you fair warning." His hips jutted forward. "Damn, you have a gifted fucking mouth."

I moaned at his words, my tongue sliding around his hard shaft. My nipples brushed against my bra reminding me that I needed a little release of my own and I pushed my thighs together trying to ignore it.

Rand's hands gripped my hair tighter. "Oh fuck." He groaned and then suddenly he came with a shuddering cry. I grabbed his thighs and heard myself whimpering as I swallowed his spurting cum.

Holy fuck, that was hot.

Rand leaned back against the wall as he caught his breath and I watched his chest moving up and down. "Jesus Christ, Brooklyn." His eyes were closed but a smile started to slip up his face. "I thought you said you weren't good at oral?" His eyes popped open. Then the buzzer went off in the kitchen. "Oh, son of a bitch." He tucked his dick into his pants before zipping them up. "Cock blocker." He chuckled under his breath as he moved to go turn it off.

I stood up as Rand took the food out of the oven. It was nice to have a man in the house. A man that cooked and cleaned up after himself. When Cooper and I bought this house, it was more for me. He hardly ever spent any time here with me and when he did, well, I always felt like he wanted to be somewhere else.

"Where'd you disappear to, darlin'?" Rand interrupted my thoughts.

"Nowhere, sorry." I smiled up into his baby blues.

Rand's hand came up to touch my chin, his finger grazing my cheek. He tilted my face to the left then the right and then up just a little. "Do you want me to eat that sweet little pussy now or after we eat?" Laughter danced in his eyes.

I blushed at his dirty words. "Rand."

"Are you playing shy now, Brooklyn?" Rand's hands dropped down to my hips. "You just gave me an amazing blowjob in your hallway without even thinking about it." He pressed me against his hard chest. "It's my turn to make you feel good." His mouth was tender when it touched mine before Rand broke the kiss to nibble on my bottom lip. Then he picked me up and placed me on the kitchen counter.

"Rand!" I exclaimed. "Are you seriously going to—" His lips were on mine again, devouring my will to resist.

"Relax, darlin'. Let me do this for you." Rand's hands were on my shorts, tugging them down my hips. "Up just a little." He tapped my hips for me to lift up so he could remove them the rest of the way, dropping them on the floor. I felt Rand's fingers tracing the edge of my panties. "You're always so fucking wet and ready for me."

I moaned and arched my hips as Rand's finger traced the wet spot on my underwear. "Rand, don't tease me," I begged him.

"Now you want this?" Rand's hooded eyes met my brown ones. "Tell me." He cupped my sex in his hand. "Tell me what you want, darlin'."

I blushed again before I bit down on my lip. "Touch me," I whispered softly. "Touch me and make me..." I nearly screamed when I felt Rand's finger brush against my wet folds. He had just pushed aside my underwear like they weren't even there.

"Was that so hard?" Rand teased. He smiled up at me before he leaned down and started to explore with his tongue.

The bold swipe of Rand's tongue sent my head spinning. I cried out his name before digging my hands into his hair tightly. Rand's tongue swirled against my clit as my thighs clenched around his head. His tongue never stopped working my center and I could already feel the hot fire starting to build up my hips and spine. I begged Rand to keep going. I begged him not to stop and when he worked a finger inside my aching heat, my orgasm hit me like a truck.

My muscles spasmed around Rand's finger as pleasure rocketed through my body. My toes curled and my back arched at the same time. It felt like every inch of my body was alive with energy until I slumped back against the cabinets.

"Told you I'd make you feel good, darlin'."

I opened my eyes to find Rand standing in front of me again. I felt a lazy smile spread across my face. "I might die if you keep doing that." I took his hand when he held it out to help me off the counter.

Rand chuckled softly. "There're worse ways to die." He slapped my ass lightly when I bent down to get my shorts. "You have a fantastic body, Brooklyn. Did I tell you that yet?"

I stared up at him. No one had ever told me that before. I mean, sure, Cooper had told me I looked nice when he needed to, but not when I wanted him to. Not when we went to the awards banquet and I had found what I thought was the perfect dress. The one that cost way more than I could afford, but I wanted it anyway. He didn't even say a thing. I pretended not to care, but deep down, I was so upset that I swore I would never buy a dress like that again. Until we had to go to a wedding for another driver and he scolded me for buying a dress that he didn't think was sexy enough.

"I lost you again." Rand's voice interrupted my thoughts. "Are you alright?"

I blinked away tears that I didn't even know were in my eyes. "I'm fine." I smiled up at him.

"Hungry?" he asked before turning back to the food in the oven.

"Starving." I watched him for a second. "Rand—"

"Yes, darlin'?"

"Thank you." God, he was too much. He put on this bad boy attitude, but he wasn't like that at all.

Rand found the plates and turned back to face me again. "For what?"

"Cooking. Giving me a ride home. For—" I swallowed hard.

"Offering to buy me a car." I smiled at him shyly. "You're not such a bad guy."

"Don't tell anyone." Rand winked at me. "Come on, darlin', let's eat."

***

After we ate, Rand insisted that we go for a swim in my pool. I hardly ever used it. It came with the house and I wasn't a big swimmer, so it usually just sat there most of the summer without anyone in it. It did, however, give me a chance to show off the new bathing suit I bought.

"You're fucking kidding." Rand growled at me when I took off my shirt. "That's a bathing suit?" His eyes wandered over my body before they finally landed back on my face. "Darlin', that's hardly a scrap of fabric."

I giggled. "Says the man wearing his boxers." I sat down on the edge of the pool. "Is that why you have them? So you can swim in them?" I teased.

"That is the smallest suit I have ever seen in my life." Rand moved to sit down next to me. "Seriously, I'm glad no one else can see you in that. I'd have to cover you up."

"So... does that mean you like it or you don't like it?" I slipped off the side of the pool into the water. I liked that Rand was getting a little jealous—I wasn't used to that. Cooper never cared one way or another. Maybe that's why I was so close with his brother. Even though I loved Finn like *he* was my own brother.

"What?" Rand exclaimed before jumping into the pool after me. "Get over here." He lunged at me and I squealed with laughter trying to get away from him. "Don't run from me, Brooklyn! This is not going to work in your favor. I'm bigger and faster than you are!"

He was right. I was small, with little legs and he was—well, Rand was a powerhouse whose muscles had muscles. I wanted him to catch me anyway. I want those big tattooed arms wrapped around me. I wanted to feel his chest against mine and I wanted those perfect pink lips to kiss me. Over and over again until I couldn't think of anything else.

Rand's hands suddenly grabbed me and he pulled me against him. "You didn't really put up much of a fight, darlin'." His southern accent sent chills up my spine. "You wanted me to win, didn't you?"

"Can you read my mind, Rand Shepard?" I placed a hand against his chest.

"I want to peel this bikini off of you when we get inside," Rand growled. "Then lick every drop of water off your body before I fuck you." I could feel his erection pressed against me. "How does that sound?" His hand slid up my stomach and then behind my back. "Unless you want me to fuck you right here in this pool?"

A low whimper escaped from my mouth as my other hand moved to grip his shoulder. Why did that sound so naughty and hot at the same time? I pressed my lips against Rand's chest. "Yes," I whispered softly.

Rand's started to untie my bikini top. "You are a dirty girl, aren't you?" The cool water hit my nipples as they spilled eagerly out of my bathing suit. Rand ran his fingers over them lightly making me whine at his touch. "You are so fucking beautiful."

When I looked up into Rand's blue eyes, I knew I was in trouble. There was no doubt that I was in love with him. It didn't matter that I had only known him for such a short period of time; I was head over heels for this man. I captured his lips, kissing them, sucking them, nibbling them. I couldn't get enough.

"Rand..." I tugged on his briefs, pulling them down before doing the same with my bathing suit bottoms. "I need you."

Rand grunted when I wrapped my legs around his waist, bringing him closer. He cupped my face with his big hands as I started to ease down his shaft. He felt so big—*too big*—like I always thought when his cock started to fill me, but my pussy just seemed to stretch and devour him.

I moaned as we started to move together, our bodies moving like one. I could feel his dick dragging along me as I arched my hips to meet Rand's strokes. God, sex had never felt like this before. I whispered his name as I clung to his shoulders, begging him to go slower. Fuck, it felt so good. He felt so good inside me.

Rand's fingers dug into my hips as I rode him. "Brooklyn, I don't know if I can last much longer," he warned me. "It's too... you feel too good." He bit down on his bottom lip when I started to slowly roll my hips in circles against him. "Fuck... I'm going to come."

I wrapped my arms around Rand's neck as we came together in cascading waves. Every inch of my body was alive with savage energy as I slowly rode out my climax. Rand's mouth swallowed my cries as I squirmed against him, his body tensing and shuddering beneath me.

I stayed against Rand for what felt like forever even after he had pulled out of me. My body felt completely drained. I knew he was going to have to leave soon. I knew he had a race this weekend and I wondered when I would see him again. I looked up.

"You alright?" He smiled at me. "What's wrong, darlin'?"

"Where is the race this weekend? I thought maybe if it's not too far away—" I stopped to chew on my bottom lip. "Never mind."

Rand tucked a finger under my chin. "Are you saying you want to come to the race with me this weekend?" His eyes searched my face.

"I thought I could come down for the weekend." I placed my hand against Rand's chest and started tracing one of his tattoos. "I mean, if you wanted me to."

"Hey." Rand tilted my face back up to look at him. "I would love for you to come to a race. I was thinking the same thing since I have to leave tomorrow."

My face fell. "You do?"

"I know, but I have some work shit to do. Some sponsor stuff." Rand sighed. "I'll be at the track on Thursday night. That's really not that far. Only a couple of days if you make it." Rand ran his hand over my hair. "When did you want to come down?"

"I can be there on Friday, if you want me there." I was so

fucking in love with Rand it scared me. How could I hate him one day and be in love with him the next?

Rand pressed his lips to my forehead. "I want you there," he assured me.

"Can I ask you a question?" I asked softly. When Rand didn't answer right away I turned to look at him. He smiled at me with a faraway look in his eyes. "Do you know how old I am?"

"Finn might have mentioned it." Rand tucked a piece of hair behind my ear. "Why? You think that bothers me?" He tilted his head. "Does it bother you?"

"No."

"Then don't worry about it because that just makes you a cougar."

"Rand Shepard!" I slapped his chest playfully. "Eight years is kind of a big deal though."

"Darlin', I honestly don't care that you're older than me." He brought his mouth close enough to kiss me. "Now, let's enjoy the time we have while I'm still here."

Chapter Twelve
RAND

I wanted to run. I probably should. I felt like this once before. It nearly ruined me. But, I knew that Brooklyn was different, that she wouldn't break my heart. Brooklyn was pure and perfect. When she told me she wanted to come to the race this weekend, it scared the shit out of me. I wasn't used to this relationship thing. I had never been in one before.

Crazy, right? At twenty years old, a guy should have had at least a couple of serious girlfriends. Or at least a girlfriend or two, even if they weren't too serious. But, good old fucking Nora made sure to ruin that for me. The thought of dating never entered my mind after she ruined my fucking life. But now? Now I wanted it all.

The house. The picket fence. The two-point-five kids. Fuck, toss in a dog or two while you're at it. If Brooklyn wants it, I'll have whatever she's having.

I sighed and tightened my grip on the sleeping woman in my arms. I was supposed to be sleeping, too, but that wasn't going to happen.

After our little session in the pool, I decided to take my girl—Jesus I loved how that sounded—on a real date. Nothing serious, but seeing that I wouldn't be able to see her or hold her or anything until Friday, I wanted to spoil her. Just a little.

Then of course, I remembered Brooklyn didn't have a car. This meant I had to figure that out. I was able to get a rental, which I secured for a few days. So she would have a car. I was still annoyed that Brooklyn wouldn't let me buy that car for her. I texted Ethan about the car and told him to get it ready anyway. She needed something. I'd deal with whatever Brooklyn threw at me.

Brooklyn took me to her favorite Italian restaurant. I enjoyed seeing where she grew up and she still loved living in that same town. I saw the looks she was getting when people saw her with me, but Brooklyn didn't seem to notice or care. I couldn't tell if it was my tattoos or the fact that she was with another man. Maybe it was both. Either way, fuck them. Cooper had been gone for nearly two years. Wasn't the woman allowed to start dating again? To be happy?

The food was outstanding. I could see why Brooklyn liked it so much. I finished my entire meal and then what she didn't finish, which she thought was hilarious. I did like the fact that she did actually eat though. Brooklyn was the type of woman who wasn't afraid to eat in front of a man and that was perfect for me.

Brooklyn was pretty damn perfect.

I asked her a lot about her youth, about what it was like growing up. I know she mentioned her grandparents raised her, so I didn't mention her parents. I understand what that was like. Having shitty parents. I was surprised when Brooklyn told me she was a bit of a troublemaker, even after meeting Cooper. She said she was angry at the world until she discovered her love of photography.

I talked about my childhood when she asked. I know that Brooklyn was curious about my upbringing, but I didn't like to talk about it. She asked questions, but not enough to annoy me. I normally hated to talk about myself, but I was used to it with my career. Brooklyn asked about my parents and, as usual, I lied. She would never meet them anyway. I would make sure of that.

Every time Cooper's name was mentioned I had to remind myself it was wrong to speak ill of the dead. That fucker had never deserved Brooklyn. I was sorry he was gone, but he treated her like shit. Didn't he know what he had? Bastard.

After we ate, we went to see a movie. It was literally the smallest theatre I have ever been to. It had two movie screens and the box office was outside. Like some old-timey shit. I got popcorn and Brooklyn had Sno-Caps. We saw *Avengers: Infinity Wary* which I had been dying to see. It was as awesome as I thought it would be and I was thrilled beyond belief when Brooklyn told me she loved it, too.

When we got back to her place, Brooklyn was all over me. Not that I wasn't all over her, too. Her soft curves and amazing tits drove me insane. We hardly made it through the front door before Brooklyn had my pants down in the front foyer, her plump lips wrapped around my cock. Fuck, just thinking about that made me hard again. I fucked her right there against the wall while she cried out my name.

Jesus, I loved when Brooklyn said my name. It was sexy as hell.

Brooklyn smacked her lips together while she slept and rolled over to face me. Fuck, she was beautiful. I saw the way that other men looked at her even if she didn't. Not that I blamed them. The moment I saw her I felt the same way. The big brown eyes, the dark hair. Curves that went on for days. I totally fucking got it. They just had to make sure I didn't catch them staring *too* fucking long.

I must have dozed off at some point because the alarm woke me, and I found myself alone in Brooklyn's bed. For some reason that bothered me. Reaching for my girl and finding her gone. I found her in the kitchen with her cell phone attached to her ear.

Brooklyn's eyes lit up like the sun when she saw me, and she put her finger up to let me know she'd be just a minute. *Right.* I moved behind her and pressed my morning wood against her backside and wrapped my arms around her small frame.

"Finn." The way Brooklyn's voice went up when she said that fucker's name was worth it. "I'm fine. How many times do I have to tell you? You don't have to worry about me."

Did Finn know I was at her house? Did Brooklyn tell him we were together? What did he think of that? I'd make sure he fucking knew she was mine.

"I'll see you on Friday. Yes, I love you, too." Brooklyn hit end on her phone. "Rand!" She giggled as she tried to get out of my arms. That only made me hold her closer.

"Good morning, darlin'." I lifted her off her feet so I could bury my face against her neck. She always smelled so good. Today it was cinnamon. "Good thing I have to leave or I'd bend you over that kitchen table right now." I felt the way Brooklyn trembled in my arms. Fuck, Friday seemed so far away.

Brooklyn twisted around to look at me once I placed her back on her feet. Her hand came up to my face and she ran her finger across my bottom lip. "Can I tell people that we're together? I mean, we are, right? Dating, I mean?"

My heart started pounding so loud in my chest that I was sure that Brooklyn could hear it. "Of course." We were. It sounded so strange, but I liked the sound of it. "You're my girl, remember?" I pressed my lips against hers as Brooklyn wrapped her arms around me as a strange feeling started to seep into my body.

I wasn't sure what it was. I had never felt it before and I quickly pushed it away so I could spend a few more hours with my girl before I had to leave her. Until Friday.

***

Leaving Brooklyn behind in Connecticut was hard. Making it through until Friday to see her was hard. Not breaking Finn's fucking face when I saw him was even harder.

I was lucky I didn't have to see him until Thursday night. I did what I had to do when I got back to North Carolina. My sponsors were important to me, just like my fans. And I wanted to make them happy. I smiled for pictures, signed autographs until I felt like my hand was going to fall off and when it was done, I called my girlfriend. Because I fucking missed her.

Walking into the garage on Thursday, I was fine. I was probably happier than I'd been in a long damn time. Until Finn jumped in my face. He just appeared out of nowhere like some sort of fucking spider.

He's lucky I didn't step on him like one.

Finn's eyes were narrowed into angry slits, his hands balled into fists at his side. I'm pretty sure he would have hit me if everyone wasn't standing around watching. "You need to break this off, whatever it is," he hissed at me.

I tilted my head. "I don't remember asking for your advice." I glanced around the garage before looking back down. "Why don't you ease off a bit?" He looked like shit.

"You're going to break her fucking heart, Shepard. Then who do you think is going to have to pick up the pieces? Again? Me, that's who, I had to stand by and watch my fucking brother do it. Then when he died, I was there for her. Sully was doing just fine without you in her life. You can't possibly think you can make her happy." Finn's nostrils flared at me.

"I think Brooklyn can take care of herself, Finn." I wanted to poke the beast until it exploded, but that wouldn't be the best thing right now.

Hate blazed in Finn's eyes. "You're an asshole, you know that? I told you—" He stopped and looked up at the ceiling like he was trying to control himself. Same shithead, same. When Finn looked back at me, I could feel the anger burning off him. "I'll fucking kill you if you break her heart.

Do you understand me?"

"Are you always this dramatic?" I felt my lips turn up into a smile.

"Joke all you want, fucker." Finn leaned toward me. "I *will* hurt you. Do you understand me?" Then he turned and stormed off in the other direction.

I let it go, the way Finn was acting. I knew he was in love with Brooklyn and he was hurting. Hopefully he'd get over it and stop acting like such an asshole toward me. We were teammates and had to get along for the most part. If Ben, our car owner, knew we were fighting like this, he'd have both our heads on a spike.

I went to check out my car, talked a bit with my crew chief and decided I'd head back to my RV. Might as well take it easy before the weekend actually began. I stopped to sign a few autographs along the way. Took a few pictures, too. I needed to hear my girl's voice, though. I missed her.

"Shepard, man, how the fuck are you?"

I turned to see one of the few drivers I considered a friend in the garage, Mason Pelletier. The dude was legit. "What's up, Mason?" We fist-bumped like a couple of assholes do.

Mason grinned at me. "Hey, I was going to head out for a drink. Want to come along? Maybe we can pick up a couple of chicks?"

I shouldn't do it. But, hey, one drink wouldn't hurt. Brooklyn had already said she had plans with Mia tonight. "Sure. Sounds good." I nodded. "I could use a drink." I didn't say anything about the chick part. That wasn't going to happen.

I had all I wanted with my beautiful girl coming to visit me tomorrow.

"Awesome, man. Lake's coming, too. We'll just stop and grab him on the way." Mason smacked my shoulder as we started toward the parking lot.

Lake as in Lake Mills. He acted like everyone didn't know he was a raging alcoholic, but yet he still managed to win races. He was probably going to be the next NASCAR champion and he was Mason's teammate so they were pretty tight.

"Cool." I faked a smile. I would have one fucking drink and cut out. Head back to my RV and call Brooklyn. That was it.

I should have known better. I shouldn't have gone at all.

<u>Chapter Thirteen</u>
RAND

What was that horrible pounding noise and how could I make it stop. Fuck, I had way too much to drink last night. The last thing I remember was Lake buying another round of shots—

"Shit!" I tumbled off my bed. What time was it? I was supposed to pick up Brooklyn. I grabbed my cell to see I had ten missed calls. And I had overslept. "Fuck!"

I stumbled out of my room, happy to see I was still wearing my clothes from last night. At least I had only fucked up halfway. Mason was passed out on my couch. Fucking fantastic.

"Shepard? Are you in there?" The pounding on the door started again.

Finn. That prick.

I nearly ripped the door off the hinges. "What?" I growled at him. Jesus, it was bright as fuck outside right now. I shaded my eyes as I glared down at him.

"You have got to be kidding me right now," Finn spat back. "Are you hungover? Well, get your shit together because Sully is on her way here. To be with *you*, asshole. I made up some bullshit excuse about your phone being dead." He poked me in the chest. "I warned you once."

I grabbed Finn's wrist. "Don't you fucking start." Then I saw her. Walking toward me like a dream dressed in a loose-fitting tan tank top and matching shorts. She might have been little, but I swear her legs went on for fucking days. I immediately dropped Finn's hand.

"Rand?" Brooklyn looked unsure of the situation. "Are you alright?" Her eyes moved behind me.

"Damn." Mason whistled softly.

"Eyes to yourself, motherfucker," I warned him.

Mason chuckled. "Now I know why you turned down those chicks last night." He held up his hands when I looked over my shoulder. "I get it, I'm leaving." He patted my arm as he pushed past me. I heard him mumble something to Finn on his way past him.

"Darlin', I am so sorry." I took a step toward her but when she took one back, my eyes shot toward Finn. "You can go."

Brooklyn shook her head. "He stays. Rand, where were you?"

Fuck. Fucking fuck.

"Can we do this inside? Please?" I would beg if I had to. "Where is your stuff?" The hurt in Brooklyn's eyes was too much. "Please, darlin'?"

She looked at Finn. "I'll just be a second."

The hell she would.

I moved so Brooklyn could walk past me before shutting the door in Finn's fucking face. When I turned to look at her,

Brooklyn was looking around. "I need to clean—"

"You promised." Her voice sounded different. "You said you wouldn't make me out to be a fool, Rand." Brooklyn's eyes landed on a half-empty beer bottle before she lifted them to me. They were full of tears.

"No—"

Brooklyn shook her head. "So, you what? You were sleeping one off? Instead of picking up your *girlfriend*?" The way she said girlfriend made me hate myself more than I already did. "With Mason? Who else? A couple of skanks? I know how this goes. I've been down this road before." She ran her hands over her arms like she was trying to warm herself up. "I won't do this again."

"Are you going to let me explain?" I wanted to touch her. Just hold Brooklyn in my arms to make her see that I was sorry. "Please?"

For a minute I thought she might say no. But Brooklyn nodded, keeping her eyes on the floor.

"No skanks," I blurted out just so Brooklyn would turn those chocolate eyes back on me. "Darlin', I'm sorry. I went out to have a couple of beers with my friends and, well. I drank too much. I fucked up." I ran my hand over the back of my neck as I sank down onto the couch. "I don't blame you for being upset."

Brooklyn took a step toward me. "No skanks?" Her lips turned up slightly. Then she surprised me by climbing onto my lap. "I was worried about you, Rand." Her fingers came up to trace my jawline, across the stubble I hadn't had time to get rid of yet.

"I'm an asshole." I really was. I didn't deserve Brooklyn. Not one bit. "I missed you, darlin'." The feeling of her fingers on my skin made my cock come alive. "I fucked up and I'm sorry."

Brooklyn brushed her lips against mine. "You're not an asshole, Rand." My name on her lips was the only thing I wanted to hear.

"Stay with me?" I wouldn't fight her if she said no.

Brooklyn shifted on my lap before searing her lips to mine. My hands found her hips to hold her in place while she dug her fingers into my shoulders. Our tongues twisted and turned together as she rubbed herself against me. "Rand." Her voice was a breathy whisper.

"You know how much I love it when you say my name, darlin'," I teased her.

"Are you two done?" Finn interrupted. I knew I should have locked the damn door. "Shepard, we have practice." He sounded beyond irritated.

"In a minute." I ran my thumb across my girl's cheek. "Yes?"

Brooklyn nodded. "Yes."

***

SULLY

Finn thought Rand was lying. I knew he was angry with me. Jealous, even. Now that I realized that Finn was in love with me, I wondered if he might be trying to sabotage my relationship with Rand.

I hoped that wasn't the case. Finn was like a brother to me.

I hated to admit the things that were going through my

head when I didn't hear from Rand last night. When I got back from Mia's and he didn't call. Or text me back when I texted him. But, I knew he was busy. So I let it go.

I missed Rand's voice. The way he called me 'darlin' when I answered the phone. That sweet southern accent made my panties wet every single time.

It got worse when I didn't hear from Rand in the morning and I started to panic. His reputation got the best of me and I called Finn. I had no one else to call and I made him go to the RV first. He had begged me not to come to the race. Finn told me that Rand was bad for me—that he'd only break my heart. He swore that he only wanted the best for me.

I almost told Rand to forget it. That this relationship thing was obviously not going to work. But then I saw how guilty he looked and how terrible he felt. It was written all over his face.

Besides. I was already hopelessly in love with the man.

I watched Rand qualify for the race later that day. He had been busy ever since that morning and I hadn't been able to see him. Which, I understood. It wasn't the first time I had been down this road. I had brought my camera with me and I took it out to take pictures. I didn't want to seem like I was hanging around and watching Rand, so I made sure to keep busy with other things, too.

As I made my way back to Rand's RV—with my bag that I had just taken from Finn's—I couldn't wait to spend time with him. This felt different than when I was with Cooper. He always seemed annoyed when I was around and not in the least bit happy to see me. No matter how many races I attended, I always regretted it. I was supposed to be Cooper's fiancée, but never felt wanted.

"Well, well, look what the cat dragged in."

I had been so busy in my own little world that I hadn't even realized that Travis was standing outside his RV. I tried to ignore him and keep going, but he grabbed my arm. "Let go." He was gripping my arm so tight I was afraid he would leave a mark.

"How's Shepard?" Travis asked, pulling me closer. "I hear the two of you are extraordinarily cozy these days."

"I don't think that's any of your goddamn business." I tried to pull my arm out of his grasp but that only made Travis grip my arm tighter. "You're hurting me."

Travis let his hand travel down between my breasts. "Such language coming out of your pretty little mouth." He put his lips against my ear. "I bet Shepard likes it when you talk dirty, doesn't he?" He chuckled softly. "You two lovebirds should watch yourselves. Don't think I've forgotten about what he did to me at my fucking party." He let go of me, giving me a hard shove.

I stumbled over my own feet and would have fallen if someone hadn't caught me. "I'm sorry." I looked up into the warm eyes of Lake Mills and it brought back more memories of Cooper. Those two had been thicker than thieves when he had still been alive.

"Careful." Lake smiled at me. "Are you alright?" He pointed toward my arm.

I nodded. "Sure, I'm fine." I hid my arm behind my back.

"Thanks… uh for catching me, Lake."

"That doesn't look like nothing, Sully. Did Travis do that to you?" Lake tried to walk around me but I turned around in a circle. "Let me see your arm." He tried to turn me around.

"What the fuck?" Rand's voice caused us both to turn around. "What's going on here?"

"Hey man, you might want to take a look at that bruise on her arm. Travis was manhandling her when I walked by," Lake pointed out. He raised his eyebrows and shrugged at me when I widened my eyes at him. Thanks a lot.

"Wait… what?" Rand was on me in a second. "Fuck! Jesus Christ, darlin'." He touched my arm lightly. "Let me see." He raised it up lightly and I saw the anger flash in his blue eyes. "I'll kill him."

"I'll help," Lake added. "It's the least I can do for all the shit Cooper put you through and I didn't stop it." I knew he meant well, but I knew there was plenty of shit that he and my late fiancée got into that I wasn't aware of.

I put my hand against Rand's chest. I realized he had just come from the track and had his fire suit on. Damn, he was sexy as hell. "Don't. He's not worth it. Honestly, it's nothing."

Rand gritted his teeth. "He hurt you, Brooklyn. That's not nothin'.'" His arm slipped around my waist. "I'm going to break his fucking face. That motherfucker. Five minutes, darlin'. That's all I need." He let go of me. "I'll meet you at the RV." He picked up my bag that was on the ground to hand to me.

Shit. Shit. Double shit. I hadn't realized I dropped my bag and I hoped my camera wasn't busted.

Lake gave me a look that I couldn't read as they head off to find Travis and I wondered what the hell just happened. I wasn't going to get Finn because he was already disappointed with me as it was. I just hoped Rand didn't get himself arrested or kicked out of NASCAR.

***

I was pacing the RV when Rand came back. He said he needed five minutes, but it was more like fifteen. I rushed to open the door for him, but I stopped when I saw his face. The purple welts on his cheek. The left eye that was already swollen shut. The busted lip. "Jesus Christ."

"Not exactly." He tried to smile. "Fuck, can you... can you get some ice, darlin'?" Rand moved to sit on the couch, grimacing as he did so.

I moved as fast as I could, getting some washcloths and ice, but couldn't seem to find anything to clean the cuts on his lip. Or his busted knuckles. I turned around to find Rand with his eyes closed. How the hell did we get here? I touched his arm and his good eye opened. "Rand—"

"Don't cry." He shook his head. "Honestly, it could have been worse." He tried to smile but I could tell his lip was bothering him. "Come here." He patted his lap. "Don't be shy now, darlin'." He grabbed me, pulling me down onto him. "Do you know how much I missed you?"

I lightly touched my fingers to his lip. "Travis did this?" I felt my blood begin to boil.

Rand shook his head. "Not Travis. I think it was Spencer Boland. Lake and I didn't think that there would be anyone else there." He brushed the hair from my face. "Travis won't touch you again, Brooklyn." He sounded serious as he took the washcloth out of my hand to wipe the blood off his lips. "Kiss me, darlin' before I die from the lack of your lips against mine."

I giggled. "I don't think that's possible," I teased him.

"Do you want to find out? Is that what you're trying to do?" Rand tilted his head before moving his face closer to mine. His kiss started off slowly before it began to build in intensity.

I felt his mouth, his hunger as the kiss went on. The way Rand's tongue seemed to take control of mine. The way his hands dug into my hair. The way he turned me slightly on his body so I could feel how much he wanted me.

"You're sure?" I pulled back just far enough. "You're hurt."

"I'll always want you," Rand whispered.

Chapter Fourteen
RAND

This was worse than any goddamn hangover I ever had. I couldn't see out of my right eye and my hands were busted up so bad I wondered if I should have gotten stitches. I didn't give a damn about myself though. No one touches my girl.

No one.

I hadn't expected Spencer Boland to be there when I got to Travis's RV. Lake and I were caught off guard by that. I didn't tell Brooklyn that Pete Harvey, Iggy Carson, and Chase Novak were there, too. So it was five against two. Not exactly fair now, was it?

I only wanted Travis. I got in a couple of good punches before they beat the shit out of me. Lake, too, for that matter. Luckily Mason and Finn showed up to break it up. Finn was less than thrilled, and I know he's going to have some choice words for me when I see him later.

Fuck him. He'd do the same thing for his girl. Actually, I think he was there *because* of Brooklyn. I knew how he felt about her, even if he wouldn't admit it.

It was all worth it though and I'd do it again, if I had to. Brooklyn was mine and I think Travis knows that now.

Brooklyn rewarded me with the best blowjob of my life. Not to mention amazing sex after that. Just the thought of how Brooklyn took control of everything was making my cock grow hard right now. How she peeled off her clothes and gave me a little striptease. Swinging her hips and everything. She had on these sexy little hip hugger panties with a matching bra that I wanted to rip from her body.

Goddamn, Brooklyn was the hottest woman I had ever seen. How did I ever get so lucky?

Brooklyn sucked me off first. Then she climbed on top of my lap and told me she wanted to fuck me. That she had been thinking about my cock ever since I had left on Tuesday morning. Brooklyn was always so fucking wet for me. She came nearly the second she wrapped that sweet little pussy around my dick, but that was alright. I told her to just keep going; I'd make her come again.

Which I did. I pulled that beautiful woman against my chest and fucked her slowly until she cried out my name, my cock buried so deep inside her warmth that I'm pretty sure I hit her G-spot.

I loved her. I knew that and I wanted to tell her before she left on Sunday. No—I didn't want Brooklyn to leave. I wanted her to stay with me. Move to North Carolina with me. I knew she had her sister to think about and her job. I understood that, but I'd help her. No matter how much she bitched about that. I wanted to help her.

Brooklyn stirred next to me and I watched as she opened her eyes, a smile spreading across her perfect lips. "Good morning." She brushed the dark hair from her face.

"Good morning," I answered back. "Sleep well?" I watched as she stretched her arms over her head. Brooklyn naked was the only thing I wanted to wake up to in the morning.

"Yes." She pushed her leg between mine before pulling her small body closer to me.

I ran my hand over Brooklyn's hip. Down her thigh and then back up again just watching her. I loved how her body responded to me. The way little goosebumps broke out on her skin, the way her face flushed and her eyes grew dark. I wish I had time to make her come all over my dick again.

"How do you feel?" Her voice was still heavy with sleep.

Tell her, my brain screamed at me. *Tell her you love her, asshole.* "Like I was hit by a bus." I moved so that Brooklyn was underneath me on the bed.

"It looks pretty bad." Brooklyn searched my face.

She was so perfect. I couldn't tell her though. The words were just stuck in my throat and I couldn't get them out. "I'm so glad you're here." I was though. It wasn't a lie, but it wasn't what I wanted to say to her. "I just wish I didn't have to leave you here."

Brooklyn smiled up at me. "Me, too." She touched my cheek with her hand. "You go do your thing and I'll do mine." Brooklyn had gotten a call last night asking if she could take some pictures while she was here. Which she felt was a real bonus because she was always worried about money. She wouldn't be if she moved in with me.

I crushed my lips against her plump ones and knew if I kept them there too long, we'd both end up late. But just the feel of Brooklyn's hands moving into my hair, her naked tits pressed against my bare chest was enough to make me want to bury myself inside that beautiful pussy.

"Darlin'." I panted softly. "I really can't be late." Although I might be willing to take that risk.

Brooklyn giggled softly. "I'm sorry." She sighed as I climbed off the bed. "I don't want to get you into trouble."

I shook my head, laughing as I headed into the bathroom to take a shower. When I was finished, I was surprised to find Brooklyn standing in the kitchen wearing my shirt. She held out a cup of coffee. "Hope you don't mind." She tilted her head to the side.

"No, of course not." Hard to believe that a week ago we couldn't stand the sight of one another. Or rather—I wanted to fuck her, and she hated me. Or something like that. I took a sip of the coffee while I glanced at my phone. "Shit, I have to go." I shoved my phone in my pocket. "I'll see you around the track, right?"

Brooklyn nodded. "Yes."

I planted a kiss on top of Brooklyn's head as I headed toward the door. "Darlin', I look forward to it." Then I tilted her head up to brush my lips against hers before I managed to slip outside.

***

I breezed through practice like it was nothing. Chattering on about how great my car was. Don't change a damn thing. Who was I this morning? I was a happy fucking bastard, that's who I was.

Having Brooklyn with me at practice was amazing. Knowing she was there seemed to make my car run like a dream. Like she was a good luck charm that I didn't know I needed until she showed up. I liked how she made me feel and I liked how I felt right this second. Right this moment.

I didn't care about the looks I got from the other guys. I knew they heard shit from Travis. He had a big mouth. He also needed backup to protect himself. That fucker had better watch himself or—

"Shepard, a word."

I froze at the sound of my crew chief's voice. He didn't sound too happy. I turned around to face him hoping that I didn't look too pissed off or worried. Or both for that matter.

"What in the hell happened to your face?" Wyatt exclaimed. "Does the other guy look worse?" He scratched at the awful beard he refused to shave. "Look, I know you have this whole bad boy thing going on." He used air quotes around bad boy. "But, honestly? Man, it's getting old."

I opened my mouth to tell him... well, probably to tell him off. Wyatt was a good dude, but he didn't understand me. But Brooklyn appeared in my line of vision and I lost all train of thought. I hadn't seen her since this morning and she took my breath away.

Dressed in a pair of denim shorts and one of my shirts, she was every man's fantasy. Not my own shirt, but one of my race shirts with my car on it. It was tucked in so you could see her curvy body as Brooklyn stopped to take a picture of one of the other guys. Her dark hair was piled high onto her head like she usually wore it and I could see her tuck a few pieces behind her ear as she brought the camera back down. The smile Brooklyn flashed Knox Wentworth was brief but I still hated the way his eyes moved over her body as she turned to leave.

Wyatt coughed. "Is that what's going on?" His hand came down to rest on my shoulder. "Does what happened to your face have anything to do with her?"

I choked back my anger when I looked at Wyatt. "Leave her out of this." My eyes went back to find Brooklyn, but she wasn't where I had last seen her. I scanned the garage, trying to find her, only to realize she was talking to Finn. Envy began to creep into my brain as I watched them together.

"Shepard." Wyatt moved to block my view. "You want to tell me what's going on or do I have to pull it out of you? You're not usually the type to act like this around a woman."

"Brooklyn's different," I told him. "She's…" What should I tell Wyatt? How could I explain to the man that I wanted to be everything for her, but only if she would let me? "I love her."

"That's a horse of a different color now, isn't it?" Wyatt's eyebrows shot up. "She feels the same?" He turned back toward where Brooklyn was still talking to Finn.

"I'm not sure," I answered him. My heart slammed into my chest when I saw Brooklyn turn toward me. Her lips turned into a big smile before she gave me a little wave. I returned it, praying she would walk over to me before I went to her. "I haven't actually told her yet."

"Son." Wyatt sounded serious and I tried not to roll my eyes. Wyatt was a good dude—I trusted him—but I didn't need him to tell me how to deal with my love life. I had a shitty father, which he knew about, so I appreciated what he was trying to do.

"Hi." Brooklyn's voice sent desire straight through my body without me even having to look at her.

When I met her brown eyes, I saw something different behind them. Something was wrong or she was about to drop a bomb on me that I wasn't going to like. "Hi." I moved toward her then realized I should introduce my girlfriend to my crew chief. "Brooklyn, this is Wyatt Bowers. Wyatt, my girl Brooklyn Sullivan."

"We've met." Brooklyn's voice was nearly a whisper. "Hi, Wyatt."

"It's good to see you, Brooklyn. It's been a while." Wyatt nodded. "I'll talk to you later, Shepard." He gave me a look before turning back toward my car.

How didn't I know he was Cooper's chief? Was that why Brooklyn looked the way she looked? "Are you alright, darlin'?" I wanted to hold her, I wanted to kiss her. I wanted to do something. Her body language was all wrong.

"Can we go somewhere to talk?" Brooklyn reached for my hand. "Please?" Her hand was so small in mine.

"Of course," I answered.

We found a spot outside the garage that was away from the noise and everyone else. I could see the slight sunburn that had appeared on Brooklyn's otherwise creamy white skin. The sprinkle of freckles that were now splashed across the bridge of her nose.

"Rand." Brooklyn started to speak the second we were alone. Her brown eyes looked scared. "I have to leave and I'm sorry. My sister..." She chewed nervously on her bottom lip. "She's sick and I need to go."

I cupped her face in my hands. I didn't want Brooklyn to leave, but if London was sick, I knew she wanted to take care of her. "Darlin', go be with your sister." I stroked her cheek with my thumb. "I know how close the two of you are."

Brooklyn put both her hands on my wrists. "You're nothing like they say you are, Rand Shepard."

I pulled Brooklyn into my arms and against my chest. "That's our little secret," I whispered.

Chapter Fifteen
SULLY

I hated to leave Rand so early when our weekend had just started. Especially since he had just had the shit beaten out of him. *For me.* I still couldn't believe that that had happened and that Rand had actually defended me like that.

Again.

London had a few underlying problems that I hadn't told Rand about yet. Finn knew because... well, Finn just *knew.* London suffered from an eating disorder that I thought she had under control, but clearly she didn't. I wasn't exactly sure when or why it started, but it did and it was back again.

Right now London was in the hospital and I had to go be with her as much as I wanted to be with my boyfriend.

When I stepped off the elevator at the hospital, I struck by the sounds and smell that came with it. It was just so much at once. I felt like I could never have anything good in my life without something bad overshadowing it. I knew that it wasn't London's fault, but I was still disappointed. I loved my sister and as much as I wanted to understand what she was going through, I couldn't.

I was instructed by one of the nurses at the nursing station what room my sister was in and when I found her, I had to fight back tears.

London looked so, so small. I hadn't seen her in a couple of months and she had lost more weight than I realized. She was currently hooked up to a feeding pump while she slept and my heart twisted inside my chest. I couldn't do this again. The last time it was almost too much and now I was supposed to do it again? Without anyone else? I rushed out of the room and fled to one of the waiting areas, trying to catch my breath. I could ask Harper to come because she was my best friend and I knew she would. I pulled out my phone, hoping to see a text from Rand, but I was surprised when I didn't. That was alright. I knew he was busy and again, he was young. He probably had stuff going on tonight with the other drivers.

I texted for a few minutes with Harper. Then with Finn who was just checking on London and me, too, but he didn't say that. I thought about texting Rand—I mean, he was my boyfriend—but I was tired. I was going to have to get a hotel room for a little while until I was sure that London was going to be alright. I checked her room one more time before deciding I should just go sleep for the night.

***

When I got up in the morning—alone which sucked because I wanted to have Rand next to me—I was happy to find a text from my boyfriend.

Miss your sexy ass. I wish you were here today. I

hope London is alright.

My heart flooded with emotion. The man pretended to be this hard ass when he really wasn't. He cared for me and I fucking loved him.

I miss you more, Rand Shepard. Good luck today, you sexy bastard.

I giggled after I hit send, wondering what his reaction would be. I was surprised when my phone rang.

"Darlin', don't you start with me," Rand growled into my ear.

"What?" I was so confused.

Rand sounded out of breath. "I just ran out of the driver's meeting so that I could tell you how hard I am right now. Just you telling *me* I'm sexy was enough to make me wish you were here so I could bend you over and make you scream my name."

I felt my body go all slippery inside. "Oh," I whispered into the phone.

"How wet are you right now?"

"Rand!" I felt my cheeks burn at his question but couldn't deny the ache that was building between my thighs.

Rand chuckled deep in his chest. "Fuck, you're so damn sexy." He sighed softly. "I do miss you though. How's your sister?" I could hear the sound of talking behind him.

"She's about the same." I loved how Rand didn't press me for answers or question me about London. "I'm sorry I had to leave," I added.

"Darlin', don't apologize. Look, I hate to do this, but I have to go." Rand sounded disappointed. "Call me later. Or text.

Whatever is easier."

"I will," I promised.

"I love you, Brooklyn."

I wasn't sure I heard him correctly. "Rand—"

"Don't answer me or say it back yet. I just... I just wanted you to know." Rand's voice was so soft I almost couldn't hear him. "Talk to you soon." He hit end before I had the chance to tell him how I felt.

But I loved him, too. Didn't he want to know that? Fuck it, I was going to text him back and tell Rand I felt the same. I felt like he should know that I felt the same exact way.

I love you, too, Rand Shepard.

I jumped off the bed without waiting for his answer to get into the shower. I tried not to rush, but I couldn't help myself. I could tell myself that it was the shitty hotel shower and the terrible water pressure. But, I knew the reason was because I wanted to see what Rand texted back to me. I wanted him to know that he didn't have to be afraid to tell me how he felt.

Because I felt the same way.

I was out of the shower in record time, wrapping my hair in a towel and drying off with an even scratchier one. I knew that Harper was planning on driving down to the hospital today, so I wanted to get there before she did. I wanted London to see me before Harper showed up, too. I didn't bother to do anything with my hair other than throw the wet mess into a ponytail and then I dashed back out into the hotel room.

My cell phone was blinking like a disco ball. With one text message from Harper. Two missed calls from Rand and one text.

I wanted to hear your voice when you told me that, darlin'. I won't be able to answer my phone until after the race. But I'll be thinking of you the whole time. ILY

I felt the biggest, stupidest smile slip across my face and I felt like I stared at my phone forever until it beeped at me again with another text from Harper. Oh… right.

I'll be at the hospital in about 20. I'm bringing coffee.

Shit, I need to be getting a move on if I wanted to beat her there. I texted her back to let her know she was a lifesaver before I threw on some clothes and headed back to the hospital with a smile on my face.

London was awake when I stepped into her hospital room. Her hair was exactly like mine but her eyes were blue like our mother's and they looked sad with dark circles underneath them. She tried to give me a smile, but she burst into tears instead.

Shit.

I wrapped my arms around my little sister as much as possible. "Ssshhh, it's alright," I assured London, even though I wasn't sure that I could handle this again. Every time London had a breakdown, every time I had to put her back into the ED clinic, I felt a part of her slip away from me that I knew I would never get back again. Maybe sending her to school in New York hadn't been such a good idea.

"Knock, knock!" Harper's voice boomed through the hospital room.

I let go of London to lock eyes with my best friend. She always looked so damn put together. I had never known her *not* to look good. You could call Harper at two a.m. for something and the girl would come over in her pajamas looking like she just walked off a runway stage. I'm not even kidding.

"Harper, you didn't have to come." London's voice was hoarse, which meant she'd been doing more than just starving herself this time around. Her eyes swept from my best friend to me. "Neither of you need to be here." But I saw how thankful she was whether she wanted to admit it or not.

"Nonsense, little Sullivan." Harper handed me a large coffee. "You're like family to me." She leaned in to hug London. "I'd be here no matter what."

I knew that I was lucky. Lucky to have an amazing best friend like Harper who dropped everything and drove straight here to be with me. To be with my sister. The three of us had grown up together, Harper looking after London when I wasn't around to do so. In fact, she was the one to notice how thin my sister was getting before I did. I was so caught up in my own issues—my own problems—that I had forgotten I had a sister to look after.

"I'm sure you want to know..." London looked down at her hands which were gripping the blanket covering her frail, thin frame. "What caused it? This time." I saw the tears that clung to her lashes.

"Not if you aren't ready to talk about it." I sat down on the side of the bed. "I think you should come home."

"No."

"London."

My sister shook her head. "Sully, please. I'll get the help I need, I swear to you." London met my eyes. "I'll see a therapist every single day, but I need to stay in school. It means so much to me." Her eyes pleaded with me not to take away the one thing she needed in her life.

I brushed the hair from her forehead. "I won't rule it out." I wouldn't either. But it also meant that I would be staying in New York for the foreseeable future. Just to make sure London was safe.

London threw her arms around me. "You're the best," she whispered into my ear.

"Miss Sullivan, how are you this morning?"

We all turned at the sound of the voice behind us. The doctor was young, younger than any doctor I had ever met before. His eyes were parakeet green, his hair the color of spun gold. He was tall, but not as tall as Rand. My heart suddenly felt empty without him there with me.

"I'm alright; better now that my sister is here." London managed a weak smile. I knew how she felt about male doctors and wondered if she had asked for a female.

"You must be—" I watched as the doctor looked down at the chart in front of him. "Brooklyn? London's legal guardian?" He pinned his eyes on me. "I'm Dr. Mike." He stuck out his hand.

"Dr. Mike?" Harper asked.

I took his hand. "Yes, that's me. It's nice to meet you."

"It's actually Dr. Woods, but I just use Mike. It's easier when I see the children." He glanced briefly at Harper before turning his attention back to me. "Miss Sullivan, may I speak with you alone?" He put his hand on my shoulder.

"Sure. London, Harper, I'll be right back."

We walked outside and into the hallway where I followed Dr. Mike into a small office. He turned to face me with a grim look on his face. I didn't like where this was going.

"Your sister is very sick." His eyes were serious when he spoke. "She's been anorexic now for—"

"Nearly ten years," I answered before the doctor could look in his chart. "Just tell me the truth. Is London dying?" Hot tears pricked my eyes.

Dr. Mike pointed toward one of the chairs where I moved to sit down. He sat in the one across from me. "She might, if she doesn't get herself the help she needs." The doctor sighed softly. "How involved with her life are you?"

"I-I..." I bit my lip. "I'm in Connecticut, we talk often. I can't take her out of school, it'll crush her." But if it meant that London would get better?

"Are you aware that London hasn't had a period in almost a year?"

"What?" I shot out of the chair, knocking it to the ground. "I thought... I thought that she had this under control." I felt like I was going to pass out.

"A lot of girls—and boys—with eating disorders are very good at hiding them." Dr. Mike's eyes were kind. "You're aware of the possible risks." It wasn't a question.

Of course I knew what could happen if London didn't get better. Cardiovascular disease, issues with the endocrine system. Prosthesis. *Death*. I picked the chair up that I had knocked over before I sat back down. "Has she been throwing up?" I knew that answer, too.

"Yes." Dr. Mike put the chart down. "I'm going to recommend that London be placed in Silver Hill Treatment center in Washington DC. It's one of the best hospitals on the east coast. It's the best thing you can do for her right now, Miss Sullivan."

I wanted to scream. I wanted to cry. I wanted to throw something. I couldn't afford this. London needed this treatment. "How-how much?" I dragged my teeth over my bottom lip.

"Don't worry about that now." Dr. Mike patted my hand. "We can work out a payment plan once we get her settled in." He stood up. "I'll get the papers together and we can talk to London together."

A payment plan. I suppose I could do that. London was going to be so angry with me. I was going to have to be close to her while she was staying at the treatment center. I wasn't looking forward to this conversation one bit.

***

I was drained. Physically and emotionally. After the doctor and I had told London what the next step was going to be in her treatment, she freaked out. Just like I knew she would. She cried, she screamed. She threw a few things across the hospital room. She had done all of this before. It usually worked for a few months, but her eating disorder seemed to come back harder every single time.

I promised London that I would be there for her. That I

would visit every single day. I wouldn't let her be alone. That once she was better, she could—that she would—go back to school.

London agreed.

Tomorrow London would be going to Washington DC for two months. I would have to find a cheap hotel and hopefully some photography work.

When I got back to the hotel room, I was so tired all I wanted to do was order room service and pass out on the bed. Until I opened the door and found Rand on my bed.

"Hello, darlin'." He smiled at me as he stood up. He looked—fuck, he looked amazing. Rand was dressed in a pair of black jeans and a black t-shirt with his sponsor on it. He tilted his head sideways as his hand came up to the back of my neck. "I missed you."

I grabbed the front of Rand's shirt and pulled myself against his chest as his lips found mine. Rand's kisses were slow, wet and coaxing as I poured myself into them. He angled my mouth for a deeper kiss and the longer this went on; the more everything seemed to go away.

"Rand."

"You want to talk about it?"

"I want you to make love to me."

Rand whisked me into his arms before he placed me on the bed. He was on top of me in an instant. "I love you, Brooklyn." His eyes met mine.

My entire body felt like it was on fire when I heard those words. I stared deeply into Rand's eyes.

"I love you, too," I whispered.

This time when Rand's lips met mine, as our tongues slicked together, I felt the hunger. His mouth was hot, breathy and suddenly I couldn't wait.

"Please, Rand," I whimpered as his teeth scraped against my neck. "I need you."

Chapter Sixteen
RAND

I don't think I had anything left inside me after last night. Brooklyn had been on fire, in more ways than one. She hardly gave me a chance to get my jeans off before she wrapped her legs around my waist. Brooklyn had been so fucking wet, so fucking ready for me when I slipped the head of my dick against her entrance, teasing her.

That wasn't enough though.

Brooklyn had bucked her hips and then wrapped her hand around my shaft to urge me inside. Fuck—I nearly came from that alone. I went balls deep inside her hot little pussy after that and we both came together in shuddering waves. Brooklyn's hands tugged hard on my hair as I whispered how much I loved her into her ear.

Then Brooklyn was above me. She straddled me while she eased her beautiful cunt down around my cock. The way she quaked and trembled around me was maddening. Even though I had just unloaded inside Brooklyn, I was ready to do it again. She rode me like a woman possessed and it was fucking amazing.

Brooklyn came all over my dick the second time as I sucked so hard on her nipple I was afraid I would hurt her. She insisted she wanted more. She rolled them between her fingers and moaned about how good it felt. Asked me if I wanted to touch them. Didn't I want to suck on them?

Jesus Christ, of course I did.

The third time, Brooklyn rolled over and shook her ass in my face. She looked at me over her shoulder and asked me to fuck her. Again. As I sank inside her warm, wet, cum soaked pussy, I swore my dick was so hard it hurt. I had already come twice and I was ready to do it again. As I started to move, I felt my balls slapping against Brooklyn, saw the way she fisted the sheets and the sounds she made—fuck it was hot.

Harder. More, Faster. Rand.

I came within seconds as Brooklyn writhed underneath me, crying out my name.

The fourth—and last—time was slower. We made love this time. Hot, slow kisses. We stared into each other's eyes as I pushed Brooklyn's hands up over her head before I laced my fingers through hers.

I licked and sucked all over her neck as Brooklyn did the same to mine. I whispered *I love you* and Brooklyn whispered *I love you more*. My strokes were slow, firm and possessive as they left us both tormented in ecstasy. I could easily have lost myself in her warmth, but not this time.

I could tell when Brooklyn was close this time and I pulled her up into my arms, into a sitting position. We both came hard.

It was like little bombs of pleasure as her body shuddered against mine and I swore I would never let anyone take this woman from me as I felt myself explode inside her once more.

I didn't sleep much after that. I wanted to—my body was drained completely—but I was afraid if I closed my eyes I would wake up alone in my RV. Or worse—in my empty house.

Brooklyn smacked her lips together as she slept before she rolled over onto my shoulder. I wasn't leaving without her this time. I brushed the hair from her face before twisting a piece of it around my index finger.

"Rand, what time is it?" Her big brown eyes were cloudy with sleep.

"Early, darlin'. Go back to sleep." I brushed my lips against hers.

Brooklyn wrapped her arms around my waist. "How was the race?" Her lips brushed against my chest as she spoke.

"I won."

Brooklyn's head shot up. "What?"

I felt a lazy smile spread across my face. "I wish you could have been there, it was fucking amazing." I laughed as my girlfriend—fuck, I loved how that sounded—struggled to climb up over my body and across the room. "Where are you going?"

"My phone—I need to see that," she called to me from where her phone was charging. "Dammit—I'm sorry I missed that. I should have been there." I could hear the sound of the video playing as she found the highlights from the race. "I'm so damn proud of you, Rand." Her voice cracked when she said my name.

I swooped in behind Brooklyn to wrap my arms around her. "There will be other races," I assured her.

"It was your first win."

I spun her around. "Darlin', your sister is sick. You needed to be here—hey, don't do that." I caught one of her tears with my thumb. "Brooklyn, what's wrong? This isn't about me, is it?" I tilted her head up to look at me. "How sick *is* London?"

"She's really sick, Rand. She-she has to be admitted to a special hospital and I don't... it's really expensive and I—"

I pulled Brooklyn against me. "Don't worry about how much it's going to cost. I'll take care of it." I would pay for anything and everything London needed. I would give the woman a fucking kidney if she needed one. Brooklyn struggled against me.

"Rand, I can't let you do that." She pulled back.

"Yes, you can." I watched as Brooklyn found my shirt on the floor and pulled it on. "I want to help you. I want to help your sister." I reached for her hand, but she pulled away. "Darlin'—"

"No." Brooklyn shook her head. "Don't you start that."

Fuck, here we go.

"Dammit, Brooklyn." I ran both my hands through my hair and pushed down on my neck. "I love you. I don't want you to have to struggle with anything. Let me..." I sighed. "Let me take care of you. I want you to come home with me. I want you to live with me. I *need* you. I want to marry you and make babies with you someday."

Brooklyn's eyes grew round at my words. "Rand."

"I know. It's too soon, but damn, you make me fucking happy. I'm a nicer person when you're with me. I want to be a better person because of you and—" Brooklyn put her hand over my mouth.

"Stop talking, Rand." She smiled at me with those perfect pouty lips. "I'll pay you back. Don't fight me on this."

I smiled at her. "Fine." No fucking way was she paying me back.

"Now, let's go try to get more sleep." I tried to coax her back into the hotel bed.

"I'm not sleeping anymore." Brooklyn's hand grazed my cock.

"Fuck, are you even human?"

Brooklyn giggled. "You make me an animal, Shepard," she teased softly. "Come fuck me like one."

***

After I fucked Brooklyn in the bed—and the shower—we decided to get some breakfast. It was already seven a.m. and we both realized we weren't going to get any sleep after that. I was more than happy to take my smoking hot girlfriend out where everyone could see her. To show the world that she was, in fact, mine.

There was a restaurant around the corner from the hotel and just a block from the hospital that happened to serve a killer breakfast. I was starving and I couldn't wait to dig into a stack of pancakes. Not to mention drink a gallon of coffee. I also hoped that while we were there, I could coax Brooklyn into telling me what was wrong with her sister.

I hadn't asked. I didn't pressure her. I knew that when Brooklyn was ready, she would tell me. But, I would be lying if I said I wasn't curious. It must be something serious if the doctors wanted to admit London to a different hospital in Washington DC.

Once we placed our orders—I was practically drooling over the idea of real maple syrup with a side of bacon with my meal— I reached across the table to take one of Brooklyn's hands. "I hate to see you look so sad, darlin'."

Brooklyn stirred the spoon in her coffee before she finally looked up at me. She ordered a Belgian waffle with strawberries, but something told me she wasn't even going to eat half of her meal. "London has an eating disorder." She pulled her bottom lip into her mouth. "She's been anorexic for the past four or five years." I watched as tears slipped down her cheeks. "If London doesn't get better this time, Rand, I'm afraid she's going to kill herself."

Before I even realized it, I had gotten up to slip into the booth next to Brooklyn. "She's going to get better," I assured her. "Hey." I tilted her face to look at me. "You're an amazing sister. You've already done so much for her already. I know what you're doing right now is the best thing for her." It killed me to see the woman I loved in so much pain. "I don't care what it takes; we'll get the best help for London." I wrapped my arms around Brooklyn tightly.

I would slay dragons for this woman if I had to.

"Shit, I've been looking for you everywhere, Sully." Finn's worried voice interrupted us. "Don't you answer your phone?"

Of course Finn would be here. He was the brother of Brooklyn's late fiancé. He knew London—who I hadn't met yet. I gritted my teeth together knowing I had to play nice as I looked up into his eyes. They were anything but worried. More like angry when he realized who Brooklyn was sitting with.

Mine. She's fucking mine, Finn. Suck on that one.

"How is she?" Finn's eyes moved from Brooklyn to me and then back to Brooklyn again. He slipped into the booth across from us where I had been sitting.

Sure, just make yourself comfortable. We weren't having a private conversation or date or anything. Dick.

"Bad."

Finn's eyes furrowed together. "When..." Again he looked at me.

"Whatever you need to say, Finn, you can say it in front of Rand." Brooklyn's hand moved to my thigh. Wrong time for me to get an erection, but I can't stop my dick.

Fire burned in Finn's eyes for a brief moment. "When can I see her?"

The waitress came back with our food at that moment. Seeing Finn there, she asked if he wanted anything. He didn't.

"Finn." Brooklyn cut off a piece of her waffle. "You can go now if you want. Rand and I were going to go after we ate. You don't have to wait for us." Her hand dropped back to my leg again.

Us. There's an us.

I realized that I hadn't even said anything since Finn showed up at our table. Odd for me, but I wanted to be the man

Brooklyn deserved. So I just cut up my pancakes and covered them in massive amounts of syrup before diving into them.

"Dude, that's disgusting."

I locked eyes with Finn as I finished swallowing my food. I wiped my mouth with the paper napkin before taking a sip of my almost empty coffee cup. "Say again?" I felt a smirk creeping up my face. Don't start with me, Houston. I will fucking crush you.

"All that syrup. How can you eat that?" Finn shook his head. "Don't get me wrong, man, I like pancakes just as much as the next guy, but why smother them like that?"

Brooklyn's grip tensed just slightly on my leg. Was Finn making small talk with me? Was he being nice right now? I wasn't sure I was actually awake. Maybe I was dreaming. I opened my mouth, but nothing came out.

"Next you'll tell me you like them with chocolate chips, too." Finn chuckled softly.

I suddenly realized that he was doing this for Brooklyn. Like me, he wanted to make her happy. "As a matter of fact." I popped a piece of maple covered pancake into my mouth. "I do."

"Oh, shit." Finn rolled his eyes. "Man, I don't know about that." He nodded at Brooklyn. "You sure about him, Sully? I mean..." He let his voice trail off.

Brooklyn leaned against my side. "Absolutely." She giggled. "Although, the syrup thing is a hard no," she teased as she looked up into my eyes.

"The two of you are ganging up on me now?" I laughed loud

and deep. I couldn't remember the last time I had done that. It had been a long time since I had felt like I could be myself with someone. Like I could relax and not feel like I had to be someone else.

Finn stood up. "I'll let you two finish up here. I'm going over to go check on London." He nodded and actually fucking smiled at me. Shit, did that mean he didn't hate me as much now? "I'll see you there."

"Of course." Brooklyn was still nestled into my side. "Let London know I'm on my way."

"I'm sure she knows, Sully, but I'll remind her." Finn's hand landed on my shoulder. *Hard.*

"Fuck, maybe I should have warned him Harper was here." Brooklyn took another bite of her breakfast.

I could still feel where Finn's hand had been. The warning behind it. The way he was trying to tell me that he still didn't fucking trust me. I suddenly lost my appetite.

"Rand?"

Shit, Brooklyn had been talking to me and I had zoned out. I smiled at her. "Sorry, darlin'. I'm just tired. Did you say Harper was here?" Someone else who fucking hated me. I let my hand graze her cheek.

She nodded. "Yes. Finn and Harper—they have a bit of a past together." She finished off her coffee. "I'm ready to go whenever you are," Brooklyn added.

I stood up to let Brooklyn out of the booth and grabbed her hand as we headed out of the restaurant before we started our walk to the hospital. Finn and Harper? That was something I couldn't picture. But here I was with Brooklyn, so who was I to judge?

The hospital was right across the street, so we made our way to London's room. I wasn't nervous about meeting Brooklyn's sister. I was worried about how my girlfriend's sister would react to meeting me.

"Ready?" Brooklyn squeezed my hand just before she knocked softly on the door.

Chapter Seventeen
SULLY

When I walked into the hospital room with Rand, I expected to see London. Not Harper and Finn making out like a couple of fifteen-year-old kids at a drive-in movie. I'm pretty sure Finn had had his hand up my best friend's shirt, too, but I turned away before I could see something I didn't want to.

Rand started laughing. Like it was the funniest thing he had ever seen in his entire life. I was horrified. Not to mention embarrassed.

"Jesus Christ! Could you knock?" Harper exclaimed.

I whipped back around. "Could *I* have knocked? Harper, this isn't your room. I can't believe you two!" I hissed between clenched teeth. "This is a hospital, not a fucking porno." I was so mad right now I wanted to punch something. Until I saw the look on Rand's face.

I knew Rand was worried about Finn liking him. Whether he wanted to admit it or not, Rand wanted Finn to accept him. He knew Finn was like a brother to me. Right now Rand had the biggest shit-eating grin on his face while his eyes were glowing with happiness.

"Sorry, Brooklyn. I know you're mad, but this?" He waved his hand at Finn and Harper. "This is fucking classic." He let out another belly laugh.

My boyfriend didn't laugh like that enough.

I put my hand over my mouth. "Stop." But I let a smile slip over my lips.

Finn looked like he wanted the floor to open up and swallow him whole. He hated to be embarrassed. He only liked the good kind of attention. Winning a race? That's what Finn would love. Not something like this.

Just at that moment, London was wheeled back into the room by a nurse with Dr. Mike right behind them. I was happy to see she had a little more color in her cheeks and her eyes looked a little less sunken in. She didn't look too happy to see me or anyone else, for that matter.

"Well, look who's here," she muttered as her eyes swept through the room. They stopped on Rand. "Do I know you?" I didn't like the way London was staring at him. I hadn't had the chance to tell my sister about Rand yet with everything that had been going on. I mentioned that I had met someone, but that was as far as it went. Her eyebrows shot up. "Holy shit."

"London." I wasn't about to have this conversation now.

Dr. Mike coughed softly. "Brooklyn, can I talk to you?" He tilted his head. "I need to go over a few things."

I reached for Rand's hand. "Of course." When I turned to meet his eyes they looked... well, they looked almost scared. We followed the doctor back to the same office I had spoken with him in yesterday and after introductions, sat down to find out how London was doing this morning.

"So." Dr. Mike placed his hands on the desk in front of him. "London is very…" He gave me a small smile. "Very stubborn. That being said." He picked up the chart for a moment and I squeezed Rand's hand. His silence was starting to scare me. "She's doing better, even after only a few days."

"That's good."

"Very." Dr. Mike nodded. "There will be an opening this afternoon at Silver Hill. London is very resistant on going, as I'm sure you're aware."

I was. London was not a fan of inpatient treatment for eating disorders. "Yes, but she promised this time she was going to stick with it." I looked up and over at Rand who had a faraway look in his eyes. Now I was really freaked out. Was he going to be able to handle this? Cooper always tried to stay out of London's ED which is why Finn was such a big part of her life.

"I have her transfer papers ready."

I looked down at the papers that were pushed in front of me. I knew that this was the best thing for London. That this was the best hospital and care for her. I signed, initialed, and dated all the spots that were indicated while chewing nervously on my bottom lip.

"Well, that's it." Dr. Mike clapped his hands. "We'll get an ambulance ready for transport for London for this afternoon." He stood up.

I felt a sense of relief wash over me as I went to go back to see my sister. I felt like things were finally going to come together, that London might actually get better.

"Brooklyn, I need to talk to you." Rand's voice sounded almost like someone else's.

I turned to look up at him. "Right now?"

"Yes, right now. I need to tell you something before we go back to see your sister."

Why wasn't Rand looking at me? He was looking behind me. Next to me. At my feet. Shit... he was even looking at my tits, but *not* in my eyes. "Rand?" I reached for his hand.

Rand ran his hand up through his hair as he shifted his weight from one foot to the other. "Look... uh... you know, before I met you..." His blue eyes were the color of the sky right now. "I slept with more women than I should have. I'm pretty sure that I slept with one of London's friends. I don't know if I did or not, but she looks really familiar. Your sister, I mean."

Wait. *What?*

I suddenly felt sick to my stomach. "You *think* you slept with one of my sister's friends?" I tried to pull my hand out of Rand's but he was too strong. I struggled anyway. "How-how do you not know who... I..." I felt my breakfast churning in my stomach. "Please let go of me."

"Darlin'."

"Rand." We locked eyes and I saw the hurt behind them. I saw how scared he was, how worried. But, what about me? Rand expected me to go into that room with him right now? When he let go of my hand, he took a step toward me. "Stop." I held my hand out.

Rand stood there for a second and I watched as emotion

after emotion flew over his gorgeous face. Until it seemed to turn to stone. "I'm leaving."

I shook my head. "I don't want you to leave; I just can't talk about this here. Rand... wait!" He was already headed toward the elevator. Seriously? I wasn't going to fucking chase him. That wasn't who I was. Instead, I went into my sister's hospital room even though my entire body was shaking.

***

They transferred London to the ED hospital that afternoon just as Dr. Mike said they would. I went back to my hotel room to find that Rand was gone. I was stunned to say the least. I didn't understand what I had done wrong. After all, he was the one that confessed to me he thought he had slept with one of London's friends.

The thought made me want to scream.

Rand said I was *his* girl now. That he was my guy, too. So, I shouldn't get upset. Sure, I could be jealous I suppose. I just didn't understand why he left like that. He should have stayed so that we could talk about it. I really needed him right now.

I had Finn and Harper to lean on of course, but that wasn't what I wanted. Finn wasn't going to stay after what happened with Harper earlier. After all the times my best friend said she wouldn't date a NASCAR driver.

I closed my eyes trying not to have a meltdown. I had sworn off drivers again and look where that had gotten me? A manwhore of a boyfriend that didn't want to stick around to talk about his issues. Which he had a lot of.

I finished packing up my belongings from the hotel room

and just as I was ready to leave, I saw a shirt sticking out from under the bed. I reached down to grab it which is when I realized it was Rand's. The one he had on last night. I held it up to my face before I could stop myself just so I could feel like he was here.

His scent filled my nose and I had to grab onto the mattress to steady myself. Gasoline, exhaust fumes, and whatever aftershave Rand wore penetrated my senses. Why did he have to make things so hard? What else had happened to this man to make him like this? I quickly shoved his shirt into my bag before finally leaving the room. Harper and I were going to drive down to Washington DC now so that I could try and find a hotel room that wasn't too far from the hospital.

Harper was waiting for me when I got to her car. Singing along to Blake Shelton while I tossed my bag into the back seat before I pulled my seat belt on.

"Where's lover boy?"

"Can we just go?" I picked at an imaginary piece of lint on my shirt. I waited for Harper to say something else, but she didn't. When she backed out of the parking spot and out of the garage, I glanced at her out of the corner of my eye.

Was my best friend actually *not* going to give me shit about a guy she didn't like me dating? It would go down in history if Harper let this go.

"How long have we been friends?" Harper's eyes were glued to the busy street in front of her.

I rolled my eyes toward her. "Forever." What was she up to?

"Right. Since we were kids, which means I know you as well as you know yourself. I'm just as much of a sister to you as London is." Harper glanced in the rearview mirror for a second. "You love him."

My heart leaped in my chest at her words. "Yes."

"Finn said Rand seems different with you around. It's only been a short time, but he's nicer. A little more level headed and happier. You did that to him."

I pulled my bottom lip into my mouth. I wasn't about to bring up what Rand told me earlier or any of his personal business. That was between us. "Rand is a good guy, Harp. He puts on a mask sometimes, but he means well."

Traffic had come to a dead stop for God only knew what reason, so Harper took the time to turn to look right at me. "I've never seen you so happy. When I walked in on the two of you that morning? Your face? I can't explain it." She shook her head. "Cooper didn't make you feel that way. Whatever happened today, fix it. You need Rand and he needs you. Stupid shit happens between couples."

"Says the woman who hasn't had a serious boyfriend in how long?" I teased.

"I'm serious, Sully." Harper clicked her tongue off the top of her mouth. "Now, that's all I'm going to say about it. Let's talk about something else. Like how you're going to bring me to the next race you go to so I can meet a hot guy."

"What? What about what we walked into earlier with you and Finn?"

Traffic started to move again so Harper's eyes went back to

the road. "That? That was just us trying to see if we actually had feelings for one another." Her lips turned up into a smile. "We don't, trust me. He's like a brother to me. It was really weird, too, kissing Finn." She laughed lightly. "I didn't even get wet and my nipples—"

"That's enough!" I cut Harper off before she could go any further. "I don't want to hear anything about your vagina or your tits, thanks," I exclaimed before making barfing noises. "That's why you want to go to a race? You've met drivers before."

Harper nodded. "Move, asshole," she muttered as she slipped the car into the right-hand lane. "But, Rand might know some hotter ones. I haven't been to a race in a couple of years." She giggled. "There's this one guy, Lake Mills." She wiggled her eyebrows.

"Lake? You want to meet Lake?"

Harper nodded. "Yes. He's hot."

I didn't want to ruin Harper's dreams, but Lake was kind of a pig when it came to women. He liked what he liked. Not that Harper wasn't hot. My best friend was a fucking dish. "Well, Rand knows Lake, so I'm sure I can work something out."

Harper giggled like a high school girl. "This is going to be so much fun," she told me.

"Rand and I have to make up first."

"You need to go to him."

"Excuse me?" I balked at her. "He left me. Not the other way around, Harp. I didn't push him away or tell him to go. Rand left. That's what he does when conflict arises."

Harper let out a low sigh. "Get his address from Finn. Or, better yet, I'll get it from Finn. Then? You go to his damn house and make him fucking talk to you." She pounded her hand lightly on the steering wheel. "What's the worst that could happen if you did that?"

The girl had a point. What was the worst that could happen if I did that? I would go to Rand tonight. Make him talk this out with me. Once I made sure that London was all settled in of course.

<u>**Chapter Eighteen**</u>
RAND

I don't know *what* the fuck is wrong with me.

I bailed on my girlfriend. Again. Like the fucking asshole that I am.

For some reason I let Mason convince me to throw a fucking party. I'm fucking wasted while some random girl keeps trying to rub up on me. I'm not even interested either.

"Babe." Mason shook his head. "Rand's taken." He pulled her off me again for the fourth, or maybe it was the fifth time. Her blonde hair was just a little too bleached. Her tits just a little *too* much for me.

Her lashes were caked with mascara. "What? Since when is the great Rand Shepard 'taken'?" she cooed at me while she batted her eyes.

"Since now." I finished off my beer as I stood up. My cock wasn't even interested in this girl. I really *was* fucking taken. I watched as the blonde turned her attention toward Mason.

"Mind if I crash upstairs?" my friend asked as he turned the girl toward the other room.

"Mi casa," I called out to him. Like he even had to ask. Guy slept here most nights these days. He was more like a brother to me than my real one *ever* would be.

Thank fuck Mason took care of that girl. She was really starting to annoy me. All I could smell was whatever fucking perfume she had on and it was awful—*really* awful. I needed some fresh air. I teetered on drunken legs as I headed toward the front door, making my way past a few other drivers as well as their dates for the evening. I made a mental note to try to figure out who invited that blonde. I grabbed another bottle of beer on my way out the door for the fuck of it.

It was cool outside. Cooler than I thought it should be for this time of year, but it was nice not to have it be melt-my-face-off hot, too. Like when I was in New Hampshire with Brooklyn.

Fuck. I missed her. If I kept acting the way I was, I was going to lose her before I even had the chance to really have her.

I sat down on the front steps of my porch and watched as a car started to slow down in front of the house. Great. Someone else that Mason had invited to this shit show of a party. I never should have agreed to this. He needed to get his own place so I didn't have to deal with these parties all the time. I used to enjoy them—the guy knew just the right girls to bring—but not now.

The new car found a spot to park while I watched as the girl—*awesome*—climbed out of the driver's side. Nice figure, great ass, too. It was a little dark to see what color hair she had, but-holy shit. I would recognize that fucking body anywhere. I was halfway across my front lawn before she even realized it.

"Brooklyn." I wanted to push her against the car so that I could kiss her lips until I couldn't see straight. Instead, I just stood there like a fucking jerk.

She looked up at me with the saddest fucking eyes I had ever seen in my life as she tucked a piece of hair behind her ear. "I'm sorry I just showed up at your house, Rand." She dragged her teeth across her bottom lip which made my cock spring to attention.

Now? Really? That gets you going? Everything about this woman gets me going now that I thought about it. I noticed she was wearing my shirt again. One of my shirts with my number on it. Did she buy them at the track this past weekend? Fuck, she was supporting me after what a dick I was?

"Rand?"

I realized I was staring at Brooklyn's body again. Something I seemed to do a lot. "Sorry, darlin'. I just—" I took a step toward her. "I'm so glad to see you."

Brooklyn's eyes moved from my face and back to my house. "You're having a party." Her voice was flat.

"What? No. Mason is having a party." Fuck. Fuck. Fuck. That dick was leaving tomorrow. If he ruined any chance I had at making up with her, I would kick his ass out to the curb for real. "Hey." I touched her face lightly just to turn her eyes back on mine. "Finn told you where I live." Maybe the asshole really wasn't such an asshole. I let my thumb glide across her cheek. "Fuck, darlin'. I'm sorry."

"Talk to me, Rand. Don't run from me. Why can't you do that?" Her voice cracked this time. Was she crying?

I dropped to my knees. Just like I always did for Brooklyn. *Because I was hers*. I fucking loved this woman. I pressed my face into her stomach before I wrapped my arms around her waist.

"I'm afraid," I whispered softly. "I'm afraid of what will happen if we fight. If I lose you." I felt Brooklyn tunnel her hands through my hair. "I'm sorry that I left. I'm sorry I just didn't tell you and then talk with you about it like I should have. I've never done this relationship thing before. I-I have a hard time trusting anyone. My parents are assholes, my brother is even worse, and you're so fucking perfect it scares me. I don't deserve you."

There. I fucking said it. My parents. My brother. Brooklyn already knew about Nora, so everything was out in the open. Or at least mostly.

I felt a tug on my hair which made me look up. It also caused the blood flow to increase the pressure in my dick. Not the time for that. I rested my chin against Brooklyn's stomach to see the tears on her face. Why was she crying? I jumped to my feet to brush the wetness from her face before she grabbed my hand and kissed it lightly.

"I didn't know you had a brother; I thought you were an only child." Her lips tickled my fingers as she held them against her mouth.

I guess now would be the time to tell Brooklyn the truth. The whole truth. Any alcohol that I had in my system seemed to have disappeared because I suddenly felt completely sober. "Would—" I stopped so that I could take a deep breath. This was hard for me. "Would you like me to tell you about him? About Eli? I haven't spoken to him in a very long time." The clouds had shifted slightly and I could see the way she looked at me in the moonlight. It made my heart fucking ache.

"Only if you want to."

I cupped Brooklyn's face in my hands before I brought my face down to hers. "I'll tell you anything and everything. I'll give you the moon, the stars, a million dollars, and my kidney if you need it." I brushed my lips against hers. "You already have my heart, darlin'. I stood up to my full height. "Come with me." I grabbed her hand.

We started to walk around the car Brooklyn had driven up in—which I assumed was a rental—before I moved slightly to the right. "We're not going inside yet," I told her before she could ask. "So, Eli." I didn't hate my brother, but he wasn't a person I cared for. "He's got a bit of a drug problem."

We were coming up around the side of the house. I loved my house. I worked fucking hard for this place. Made sure that I put everything I earned from racing into this house but saved some of that money, too. I wasn't done with it yet. I wanted to put a pool in and I had a garage, but I wanted maybe three or four stalls. I know it sounds fucking arrogant or whatever, but when you grow up with nothing—you want more. This house was much more than I needed. Five bedrooms, three baths, it was too much. I think deep down I wanted a wife, kids, the whole fucking thing. But until I met the right woman, I didn't realize that.

The house was my fucking pride and joy with the overhangs

and wraparound porch. It was three thousand square feet of living area that flows freely into the kitchen, foyer, and dining area. It was tucked away nicely with just enough privacy so that you had to know where I was to get here. I spent a lot of nights alone on that fucking porch, but as I wrapped my arm around Brooklyn's shoulders, I realized I wasn't going to do that anymore.

"This." I pointed to the shed in the back yard. "Was supposed to be for Eli." It had already been halfway converted into a tiny house before he went off to God knows where.

Brooklyn tilted her head to look up at me. "You had a house for him? Here?"

"I had Eli sent to rehab again for probably the fifth time. He had promised to really get his shit together. I had this tiny house put together for when he was ready. I even had a job worked out for him in town." I shook my head. "Eli was staying at a sober living home when he disappeared. I haven't heard from him since." I looked up at the dark sky. "My parents said they haven't heard from him either, but sometimes I think they might be lying."

Brooklyn's hand slid up my chest. I knew she wanted me to look at her, but I fucking couldn't. Not yet. Instead, I slammed my lips against hers so that I could taste her. Taste how sweet she was. Her mouth opened for mine and when her tongue slid inside my mouth, I growled deep in my chest.

Our mouths tore at one another without a sound. I needed Brooklyn, and I was pretty sure she needed me. There was nothing gentle about any of these kisses. There was hunger behind them that I knew only meant one thing.

I felt Brooklyn's hand on my stomach before I realized what she was doing. Her hand unbuttoned my jeans and then I felt her grip my shaft. I grunted into her mouth as she let her thumb roll across the tip of my dick. I pulled back to look at her. "Darlin'..."

"Let me do this, Rand."

I watched as Brooklyn tugged my jeans down just enough so that my cock popped out. She wrapped her slender hand around the base of my erection and began to slide her hand up and down. "Fuck." The word tumbled off my lips. "Grip it a little harder," I urged her. "That's it." I groaned when I felt her other hand around my balls and then her lips brushed against the crown. "Shit." I gritted my teeth. She didn't make an attempt to suck me off. Instead, her hands worked my cock as she used her lips and tongue just around the crown.

It felt too good. No, I'm not ready to come yet. "Brooklyn," I whispered and tried to make her stop. My body tensed up as I tried to fight the release that I knew was already coming. Brooklyn continued to roll my balls between her fingers as my sudden eruption hit me. It was violent, virile as I cried out in pure pleasure. Every single time this woman puts a finger on me, I can't control myself.

When I looked down, Brooklyn is looking up at me. Her big brown eyes are so full of love for me I nearly choke. I brush the pads of my thumbs across her cheeks. "I love you." The words I thought I would never tell anyone are so easy to tell her now.

"I love you," Brooklyn whispers back at me. She stood up before she wrapped her slim arms around me. My cock was still wet with my own release and she didn't even seem to care as she pressed even closer to me.

"Do you want to see the rest of the house? The inside? I'm about to kick these people out of my house."

Brooklyn giggled into my chest. That was my favorite sound next to the way she said my name. "I would love to."

"Then you can tell me about your sister. We're going to see her tomorrow so I can apologize to her next." I tucked my junk back into my pants before I turned my girl around, back toward the house. Once we got to the back of the house, I told Brooklyn to wait for me and proceeded to kick the entire party out.

"Sorry, fuckers! Everyone has to go. My girlfriend is here. Party time is over!" I bellowed at the top of my lungs. I went through the entire house to make sure it was empty. The room that Mason slept in I left alone. I'd kick his ass out tomorrow. I went back downstairs to find Brooklyn and brought her inside.

***

SULLY

I woke up not knowing where I was. The room was huge, the bed even bigger and then I found Rand stretched out next to me. His arms—and legs—wrapped around my body. I touched Rand's face while he slept and wondered what he was dreaming about. Wondering if he at least got some peace while he was sleeping.

We had stayed up all night talking. Rand had told me more about his brother. How at one point they actually had been super close. Eli Shepard had actually had plans to be a NASCAR driver, too. Until the drugs took over his life. Their parents hadn't been much help. Turns out they were big-time drinkers and hadn't been the best parents. Now that Rand was successful, they tried to push their way into his life.

I told Rand about my shitty parents. How my mom and dad weren't even married-not that there was anything wrong with that. It's just some people shouldn't be together. They had me first when Mom was eighteen, Dad nineteen. They moved in together and things were alright, but Dad was a bit of a slouch. He was lazy, didn't want to work. Liked to drink, too. A couple of years of that and Mom had enough. So? She left Dad, but she also left me. With my grandparents. Ten years later she came back with London. Dumped her off and she'd been gone ever since.

Last night Rand had talked about me moving here. Talked about London coming here, too. I had never wanted to come to North Carolina before. Now I thought maybe I would.

Finn and Harper were staying with London. I had to contact the clients I had back home. I had a lot to do back home. I peeled myself out from under my giant and made my way out into the hallway where I located a bathroom. Then followed the smell of coffee.

I wasn't surprised to find Mason in the kitchen. The leggy blonde next to him didn't bother me either, but the look she gave me told me she didn't feel the same about me.

"It's about time you got here, Sully." Mason placed his coffee down on the table. "I've never seen Shepard so hung up on a girl before."

I helped myself to a cup of coffee and took a sip before I finally answered him. "I had things to take care of first." It wasn't any of his business. No matter how close they might be.

"Babe, you going to sit down or what?" Mason asked the blonde. "Have you two met yet?" He tilted his head up again. "Apple, this is Brooklyn, Rand's girlfriend." He jutted a chin toward me.

Apple? That couldn't be her real name. Her blue eyes looked me over before she finally gave me a smile. A fake smile. "Nice to meet you." Her voice was breathy. Apple wasn't here for Mason, I realized. Apple wanted Rand and Rand turned her down.

"There you are." Rand's voice boomed in my ear as he grabbed me. He nuzzled my neck before he wrapped his strong arms around me. "I wondered where you wandered off to." He growled before he spun me around. "I know you have to go back to DC later, but—" Rand's eyes moved behind me. "What?"

"Nothing, man." Mason snickered. "I've just never seen you like this with a chick before."

"Mind your business, dick," Rand barked at him, but I saw the smile on his face. He tilted my face up. "Don't mind Mason, he's never been in love before. Someday he'll meet the right girl."

"Like hell," Mason pointed out.

"Get out!" Rand ordered. "Take Blueberry with you."

"It's Apple!" I heard the blonde's voice as Mason left the room with her.

Rand shook his head, but there was a smile on his face. His blue eyes danced with laughter. "Before you leave, I want to show you something."

Rand started down the hallway where we had come in from the back of the house, but stopped in front of a door. I figured it went down to the basement or was a closet. When he opened it, it turned out to be an empty room. "This could be yours." He flicked the light on. "We could put another door in over there for your clients. A walkway up the side for them to come in. A sign out front so they know where to enter. The driveway is big enough."

What? Was Rand saying this would be—

"Are you fucking serious?"

"As a heart attack, darlin'." Rand's big hands cupped my face. "Don't answer yet. Just think about it. I know this is crazy. This is so fucking fast." He smiled. A big fucking smile that made my legs weak. "I love you. I want to be with you. London can have her own room for when school isn't in session. Whatever you need."

"Rand."

"Don't say anything." He shook his head. "Just...just think about it. Promise me that you'll think about it. Take as long as you need."

Chapter Nineteen
Two Weeks Later
SULLY

Things had been crazy in the past couple of weeks.

London was doing more amazing than I thought possible. Watching her actually *want* to eat. Watching her want to get better was one of the best things in my life. Harper and Finn came by as much as they could, but they both had their own lives.

Not to mention Mia had had her babies. Two healthy twin boys that she named Noah and Neal. To say that she was a little overwhelmed was an understatement, but I think now that her mom was here she was going to be alright.

All of this meant that I hadn't had the chance to see Rand. We texted—*a lot*. We talked on the phone as much as we could, but it wasn't the same. I missed his arms around me. I missed his scent. I just missed Rand and the way he made me feel.

Get your mind out of the gutter. It's not always about sex. Even if Rand knew how to give me mind-blowing orgasms.

It was early Friday afternoon. Harper and I were making our way through the back lot of the race grounds where the drivers kept their RVs. I was nervous about leaving London— who promised she'd be fine. She felt "like a million bucks"—her words, not mine. I had my suspicions that London was actually interested in one of the other patients at the hospital, but didn't want to ask her. I hadn't actually seen her talking to anyone, but she talked a lot about how she enjoyed their company.

So what else could it be?

After London promised she would call me if she needed me, I was on my way to see my boyfriend.

Mia had also promised to call if she needed me, but like I said, her mom was there now, so I doubted she would need me for anything. I just enjoyed hearing about those cute little babies.

"Put your tongue back in your mouth," I hissed at Harper. "You're drooling. Jesus Christ, you'd think you'd never seen a man before." I resisted the urge to elbow my best friend. "Or a NASCAR driver before." So fucking weird. These guys were Rand and Finn's friends—she knew that.

Harper giggled like a high school girl. "Sully, I can't help it. I should have come with you sooner. I mean, sure. I've been here with you and Cooper a couple of times, but fuck. These guys are hot as sin." She craned her neck as we walked by Iggy Carson. "Damn," she muttered softly.

"What about Lake?"

Harper's head spun around so fast I thought maybe she was going to spit pea soup on me like Linda Blair in

The Exorcist. "Where?" Her eyes were wide.

"Wow, you are seriously in heat," I teased. "I asked you what *about* him. I never said he was here." I hadn't told her that Rand mentioned to Lake that I was bringing a friend with me this weekend. A single, redheaded friend.

"You sure Rand isn't going to mind that you're early?" Harper finally turned her eyes away from the drivers for a second.

I shook my head. "He's been teasing me all week about how he can't wait for me to get here." I felt a big smile spread across my face. I didn't tell Harper about what Rand said he was going to do to me when I got here.

"I am so glad I'm staying with Finn." Harper made a gagging noise. "I don't want to be in that RV tonight."

I opened my mouth to give her a smart ass answer back when I saw a familiar-looking blonde walking toward me. Was that... *Apple?*

"Sully?" Harper touched my arm lightly.

That was most definitely Apple. Bleached hair, dark roots, and shorts so short you could see her fucking vagina. Was Apple dating Mason now? That had to be it. So, why was she coming from the direction of Rand's RV? She didn't even seem to notice me as she pranced by with that bitchy look on her made-up face.

Harper circled around to get in my face. "You look like you're going to—" She jumped back just as I threw up all over the grass. "Barf."

Where the fuck did *that* come from?

"Let's go. I feel better now that I got that out of my system,"

I lied as I started walking again.

"Uh-huh." Harper didn't look so convinced. "Are you and Rand using condoms?" She started digging around in her purse as we moved along. "Take this." She shoved a piece of gum at me. "For the vomit breath." She added.

"Thanks." I popped the gum into my mouth after I unwrapped it. I felt like I might actually throw up again as I tried to remember if we had used protection. The first night, yes. But after that? No. How could I have been so fucking stupid?

Harper was giving me the side-eye now as we approached Rand's RV. It was nestled nicely in the back like usual. It looked like she wanted to say more, but couldn't when Rand opened the door.

"Brooklyn?" His baby-blue eyes went wide when he saw me standing there. He jumped out of the RV so fast before he grabbed me and crushed me against his thick chest. "Fuck, did I miss you," he whispered.

My feet didn't even touch the ground. "I hope it's alright that I'm early." Thoughts of Apple danced around in my head despite the fact that Rand was holding me against him.

"I'm going to find Finn," Harper announced. "Since you two don't need me anymore."

"His RV is just right over there," Rand murmured softly. "Come on, darlin', let's get you inside." He pulled me inside before I had a chance to say goodbye to Harper, his hands in my hair and his lips on mine. I couldn't think of anything else but him as his tongue snaked around my mouth while his body pressed me against the counter. "You're early." Rand finally pulled back to look at me. His bruises were nearly healed from the fight with Travis.

"I wanted to surprise you." I reached up to touch his face. "I'm glad."

My eyes caught the empty beer bottles behind him before I could stop myself. I let my gaze move around the RV. There were numerous cans, clothes, bags of chips and red plastic cups thrown around the room.

"I should have cleaned up. I'm sorry." Rand chuckled. "I'm a bit of a pig, I hope you realize that." He started to pull back to pick up some of the garbage, but not before I saw what he was going for.

The black bra. The one that was clearly not mine. I knew who it belonged to before I met Rand's eyes.

"Brooklyn."

"Why?" The tears pricked my eyes as I took a step back. "How could you? You promised me, Rand."

"I didn't do anything! I swear to you!" Rand dropped the garbage in his hands. "We had a party. Mason and I—"

I laughed, but it was bitter and ugly. "Mason. Again. Doesn't Mason have his own fucking place? Why is *her* bra on *your* floor?"

Rand hung his head and I watched his shoulders sag. "I didn't touch her, darlin'. I swear to you."

I wanted to believe him. I really did. Maybe this wasn't going to work. It was too much too soon. I couldn't trust Rand, he was too young for me. He shouldn't be tied down and should be free to date other women.

"Brooklyn—"

"We should break up."

"*What*?" Rand exclaimed.

I nodded. "We should break up. This isn't going to work between us." My whole body had started to tremble now. My insides were breaking, but I had to be strong.

"No." Rand shook his head. "I won't let you do that. I won't let you break up with me. You love me. I didn't do anything, I swear to fucking God. Why can't you believe me? Don't do this." He reached for me, but I took a step back.

"Don't make this harder than it has to be, Rand. You know you can't be a one-woman guy." Crack. That was a piece of my heart.

Rand ran his hands through his hair and tugged on it. "I told you things I've never told anyone, Brooklyn. I am so in love with you. I *need* you. I'm *your* guy." I watched as his eyes filled with tears. "You're my girl. Remember? Did-did something happen? Did someone say something because I fucking swear to you—Mason brought Apple here and I wouldn't—I didn't. Fuck!" Rand's hand came up and he knocked a row of bottles off the counter. They crashed to the floor and smashed into pieces.

My phone was buzzing in my back pocket. My head was spinning and my heart? My heart was smashed into pieces just like those bottles on the floor. I hadn't come here to break up with Rand. The man who promised me the world. The man whose world I was tearing apart.

"Please." Rand dropped to his knees. "Please, I'm fucking begging you." Big fat tears were slipping down his perfect face now. "I'll stop hanging out with Mason. I won't have any more parties. Is that what you want?"

What I wanted was to tell Rand I loved him. That I was sorry for saying I wanted to break up with him. Instead, I didn't say anything as I started to move around him.

"You're killing me, darlin', you know that, don't you?"

Don't turn around. Don't turn around. My brain screams those words at me. *Rand doesn't need you. Rand deserves something better. He's only twenty years old. What you're going to do to him—*

"You'll forget about me, Rand. Another pit bunny will come along soon enough and you won't even remember my name." I let the door slam behind me.

I could hear the sounds of bottles and who knew what else being thrown around the RV as I started to walk away, but I didn't make it too far. I collapsed onto the ground in tears where I wrapped my arms around my knees.

Finn found me, but I wasn't sure how long I had been there. My eyes were so swollen from crying I couldn't see anything.

"Did he do this? What happened?" Finn growled.

"I—no—I—" I was hysterical when I tried to answer. My body shook and I tried to hold back as a sob escaped my throat.

Finn cupped my face in his hands. "Jesus, Sully." He brushed my hair from my forehead.

"Fuck! Goddammit! Fuck!" The sounds coming from Rand's RV caused Finn to turn toward the commotion. "Piece of shit!" The door opened and a piece of furniture came flying out.

Finn stood up. "Is this because of him?"

"Let it go, Finn. Please."

"Really? Because you're out here in a puddle of tears and he's tearing his RV apart." Finn's eyes blazed with hate.

"I broke up with him." I burst into a new batch of tears at the sound of my own words. I was a fucking idiot.

Finn was back next to me. "Why?" His voice was softer now. "He loves you. I've never seen Shepard like this. I mean, not like he is right now, but when he's with you. He's different. What happened?"

I didn't want to talk about this right now. Not with the chance that any driver could walk by or anyone for that matter. "Can we go back to your RV? I'll explain there." I managed to get to my feet. I glanced over my shoulder which turned out to be a big mistake.

Rand was in the doorway with a beer in his hand and the ugliest look on his face I had ever seen.

<u>Chapter Twenty</u>
Part Two: Three Years Later
SULLY

If you would have told me that Harper would be getting married, I would have laughed in your face. If you would have told me that not only would Harper be getting married, it would be to Lake Mills, I would have called you a fucking liar. And probably checked to make sure you weren't tripping balls.

But, here we are.

Seriously, here we are. Harper and Lake are actually getting married.

Let me back things up a bit. The day that I broke up with Rand, Harper met Lake. Thanks to Rand. I thought that they would get their rocks off, have a good time, and *see you next year*.

Wrong!

They fucking loved one another. I mean, totally, completely, crazy in love. I didn't see that coming and they were so serious that Lake asked Harper to move in with him about six months after they met.

Six months after that, he asked her to marry him.

Harper took two years to plan this wedding. Two damn years! Every flower, every balloon, and every single napkin—I was so damn glad this wedding was happening today because I'm not afraid to admit my best friend had become a bit of a bridezilla.

Lake and Harper were getting married at their own home. When Harper moved down to North Carolina, Lake had been living in a small one-bedroom apartment. Now they lived on a three-acre farm with horses, cows, goats, and a couple of dogs. Not to mention the wild animals that roamed the area at all hours of the night.

"Fuck." Harper moaned as I helped her zip up her wedding gown. "I think I'm going to be sick."

"You look gorgeous, Harp," I assured her. "This dress..." I felt my eyes grow damp. "Is stunning."

It was a trumpet style gown and it was absolutely beautiful. Encrusted with beads and sequins, and finished with peaked tulle in the trumpet style skirt, it was fucking glamorous. It had a sweetheart neckline as well as a beaded illusion back that made it even more eye-catching.

It fit Harper like a glove and she knew it.

"Lake is going to die when he sees you." London giggled. My sister was doing so fantastic—she was living her best goddamn life.

I smoothed down the skirt of my chiffon red maid of honor dress. This dress was probably the prettiest thing I had ever owned in my life with the halter straps and the cascading ruffles.

I had never put on anything made by Vera Wang in my life—now I owned some.

The bridesmaids had the same dresses, but black. I was glad mine was red. Although London, Mia, and Natalie—Harper's cousin—looked good in their dresses, too.

Harper laughed. "I've been exercising my ass off to fit into this damn gown. I thought for sure I would lose a boob size before I lost anything."

"I'm just going to go take a peek and see how many people are here." I moved my way over to the door. I knew Rand was going to be here. Lake was friends with him after all. I knew he was going to be in the wedding, too. Lake's brother Spencer was the best man, so that was good, but it still meant that I would be near him and would have to take pictures with him.

Lake and Harper were getting married at their home. The entire back yard had been transformed into a wedding destination with hundreds of red and white roses, as well as black, red, and white balloons.

I spotted guests making small talk as they sat waiting. I saw a lot of drivers out there, but I was afraid to look toward where I knew Rand would be standing.

"Hey, Sully." Finn suddenly came into view. "Wow, you look, wow." His neck turned pink.

"Thanks, Finn." I reached up to straighten his tie. "You look nice, too." Maybe if things were different, I would have the same feelings he did for me. But he was Cooper's brother and it didn't feel right. Finn understood that now. We'd grown even closer over the past couple of years and he wasn't just my friend, he was my best friend.

"You alright?"

I finished his tie. "Yes, thank you." I patted his chest.

"You're making someone a little jealous," Finn said softly. "Rand hasn't taken his eyes off you since you stepped out of the room. Which is why I came over here."

"I've been trying not to make any eye contact with him." All of a sudden I felt like I had to look at Rand. The magnetic pull was too much. Like if I didn't look, I would fucking die. I let my eyes move across the room slowly until I saw him.

Rand looked—well, he looked terrible. His hair was a mess, his eyes were sunken in like he hadn't been eating and he had several bruises on his face. The second our eyes met, Rand looked away, but the damage had already been done.

My eyes went round. "Finn?" I croaked.

Finn sighed. "Do you want the long story or the short one?"

I grabbed his arm so that I could pull him back into the house. "What the fuck happened?"

"Rand's a mess, Sully. He's a train wreck, actually. He gets into fights all the time. He doesn't eat right, he drinks way too much. I'm surprised he still has a ride, if I'm being honest with you."

I did that. I broke Rand Shepard. If I hadn't left him, he wouldn't be like that. But, maybe he would because he would have—

"There you are!" Harper exclaimed. "It's almost time."

***

The wedding went off without a hitch, and I'm pretty sure

that I saw my best friend shed a tear or two during the ceremony. But I wasn't completely certain.

Now that everything was over—it was so hard for me to not be the one taking the pictures and instead being the one photographed—we were sitting down to finally have a good goddamn time.

"I am so glad that I'm finally Mrs. Lake Mills," Harper grumbled to me under her breath. "Because I am so over this wedding shit. I want to eat, get drunk, and go fuck my husband."

"I didn't need to know that last part, Harp." I laughed loudly. But, I was so happy for my best friend. She deserved everything in this world and more.

I noticed how we were all seated. Rand was as far away from me as possible. I was sitting next to Spencer, who was nice enough, but I needed to get even farther away from Rand. I wanted to get out of this tent. Out of this damn state.

At least once I had eaten and made small talk with Spencer, I was able to find Finn so that I could talk with him. We watched Lake and Harper as they had their first dance together. They looked truly in love.

"Harper and Lake look so happy," Finn pointed out.

"Because they are," I told him. The way they looked into one another's eyes. The big smiles on their faces. I never thought Harper would end up with someone like Lake, but here she was. "Hey, have you seen London?" I tilted my head around the room.

"Now that you mention it, no." Finn shrugged. "Maybe she

went to get some fresh air." His head stopped. "Um, speaking of, how about we go get some fresh air?"

"What?"

"Come on." Finn stood up.

"Are you alright? I don't want to get—" Then I saw why Finn was trying to get me outside. Rand was dancing with someone. Not just someone. Fucking Apple.

"Are you fucking kidding?" I jumped out of my chair.

Finn put his hands on my shoulders. "Don't make a scene, Sully. It's your best friend's wedding, remember?"

"Why is she here?" I wanted to punch her. I wanted to punch Rand.

"I thought she was Mason's date," Finn jumped in. "But, I don't see him."

I wanted to cry I was so mad. Instead, I sat back down. I wouldn't ruin Harper's wedding. I wouldn't. I couldn't stop watching Rand and Apple though. Fuck, I hated her. He didn't really look like he wanted to be dancing with her, so I guess that was alright.

"Hey, um, Brooklyn?" I looked up at my name to find Spencer watching me. "Do you want to dance?" He looked at Finn. "Unless this is your boyfriend? Or husband?"

I smiled. "No... I mean, yes... I mean, no, he's not my boyfriend. And, yes, I'd like to dance." Why the fuck not? He's not a NASCAR driver. He was cute, with blond hair and brown eyes. He was shy that was clear. It was only a dance. I took the hand he was holding out as I followed him to the dance floor.

If looks could kill, Spencer Mills would be a dead man with

the way Rand was looking at him. Well—fuck you. You're dancing with that skank.

"So, uh—Rand Shepard?" Spencer's voice was soft. "He keeps staring at us. Is he—? Should I be worried right now? I mean, he looks like he's already been in a few fights."

I looked over at Rand who was staring at Spencer, *not at me*, before I looked at Spencer again. "We dated. A couple of years ago." I sighed. "It didn't end well. I don't—"

"Do you still love him?" Spencer was a good dancer, which was nice. Cooper was terrible.

Yes.

"Can I interrupt this shit?" Rand was suddenly standing there, his blue eyes so angry I thought he was going to break something. That something being Spencer's legs.

"No." I shook my head. "Go back to your fruit." I turned away from him. "Leave Spencer alone, too, he's not doing anything wrong." When I looked up at Spencer, he looked petrified.

"Darlin', please-I-I need to talk to you."

"Are you drunk?" I hissed at him.

"I should-I should let the two of you talk." Spencer let go of me.

"Come with me." I grabbed Rand's hand only to feel a shock of electricity shoot right up my arm. We went outside where it was private, where we could talk and no one could hear us. Where we wouldn't make a scene. I turned around and put my hands on my hips.

Rand's blue eyes searched my face. "I miss you. I can't

sleep, I can't eat. I can't do anything."

"Is that so?"

"Her? She's here with Mason. She asked me to dance." Rand snorted.

"You said yes," I pointed out.

"You were dancing with someone else."

"Only after... we broke up," I reminded him.

Rand's body trembled at my words. "You broke up with me. I didn't want to break up. I wanted to marry you. Have babies with you. You didn't trust me."

"I'm not doing this." I turned to go back inside.

Rand's voice was like steel. "Tell me one thing, darlin'." His eyes were like ice. "Who is RJ?"

"What?"

"Don't play dumb with me, Brooklyn." Rand's voice slurred slightly. "We have a son together. A god damn son! You kept that from me. I deserve to be a part of his life."

"You-you were twenty years old. I thought—when I found out I was pregnant." I felt my head start to spin. "I didn't think you would want to have a baby. You're so young." I shook my head. "Who told you?" I had been so careful. I didn't even bring my son. He was with my grandparents back home and I missed him something awful.

Rand tilted his head. "People talk. You know, when you try to pick a fight with them. Because you're drunk, because you're a fucking idiot. Because you think you know everything."

"Finn." That bastard. He did it on purpose, too. Because he wanted us to get back together. Because he knew how much this was killing Rand. Because he knew how much this was killing me. "I'm not going to talk about this with you. Not here," I finally said.

"Yes, yes you are." Rand's voice was low and full of venom. "I have a right to know about my own damn son. Were you ever planning on telling me that we had a child together?" His blue eyes searched my face. "Answer me, goddammit!"

My bottom lip started to tremble. "Don't do this here." Everything had been so fucking hard. "Please, I don't want to cause a scene at Harper's wedding. These past few years have been so damn hard for me. I—"

Rand wasn't looking at me anymore. His eyes were narrowed and he was staring at something behind me.

"Come with me." Rand started to pull me toward the tent.

"What? No. What's going on?" I twisted my head over my shoulder.

"Inside, darlin'."

"Don't call me that, Shepard." I squealed when Rand flipped me over his shoulder. He realized too late that was what he should have done. I saw what he was trying to keep me from seeing.

London and Mason.

Mason had London pushed up against the side of the house with her legs wrapped around him. They were making out like a couple of high school kids. Oh, hell fucking no.

"What the fuck!" I screamed. They both fucking stopped to look at me. "Get the hell away from my sister!" I struggled in Rand's arms. "Put me down, asshole."

"Stop acting like this, Brooklyn. Your sister is an adult. You're acting like a child." I heard the sound of a car door open and he threw me inside before getting behind the wheel.

"You-you can't drive. You're drunk," I pointed out.

"I'm not going to drive, you are." Rand turned to face me. "I need you to calm the fuck down first." His hand came up to graze my chin. "Can you do that for me? For our son?"

His hand. His hand was still on my face. "Please stop touching me." It was too much. All of this.

Rand moved his hand. "Will you come back to my house? Talk to me and tell me about RJ? I won't try to touch you or anything, Brooklyn. I swear to you. I just... I just need you to drive the car."

I knew it was a bad idea, I never should have kept RJ from him. "Alright." I started to climb out of the car. "I'll tell you everything as long as you promise you won't interrupt me. Not once."

We switched places in the car and headed toward Rand's house.

Chapter Twenty-One
RAND

I had Brooklyn in my car and we were going to my house. This was at least some sort of start. Right?

I glanced over at her only to notice she was white-knuckling the steering wheel. "Relax, darlin'. I'm not going to murder you." I tried to get her to relax.

It didn't work.

"Stop calling me that, Rand." Brooklyn gritted her teeth. "Which way? It's been a while since I've been back to your house." She came to a stop sign and looked over at me. "Take a right," I told her. This wasn't going to be easy. I knew that. Brooklyn had broken up with me so fast two years ago that I lost myself. I nearly lost my ride, too. I was walking a tightrope right now and needed to get it together if I didn't want to get fired. "Another right," I informed her.

I was pissed at Brooklyn. Actually, furious as hell might be a better way to describe how I felt. We had a child together and she didn't think I would want to know. Because she thought I was too young? What kind of shit is that? When London had told me— "Right here, darlin'." I didn't care if she didn't want me to call her that. I was still madly in love with this woman. I hadn't even touched another girl since she left me. I couldn't nor did I want to.

Brooklyn parked the car and turned her chestnut eyes on me. "Stop it, Shepard."

"Nope."

I watched the way her nostrils flared. The way she tried to keep her anger from boiling over. "You wanted to talk. Let's talk," Brooklyn hissed at me.

"Inside." I unbuckled myself and climbed out of the car. "Don't make me carry you inside because I will. I don't think you can run too far in that dress or those heels," I added before she thought about running.

Brooklyn didn't say anything as she grabbed her little purse and marched ahead of me. Fine by me because it meant I got to watch her ass as she did. Fuck me if Brooklyn didn't look breathtaking in that dress. It hugged her in all the right places. The moment I had seen her wearing it all I had wanted to do was rip it off of her. Bury myself so deep inside her pussy that—

"Rand?" Brooklyn had her hand on her hip.

I was also hard as a fucking rock right now. "Sorry, I was lost in my own thoughts. You have the keys anyway." I watched as Brooklyn's eyes moved over my body and yep, she totally looked at my dick. Whatever, it's nothing she hasn't seen before. She'll see it again, too, believe me.

"God, I can't fucking breathe in this damn thing." I started to loosen the bow tie around my neck. "Hey, where do you think you're going?" I called after Brooklyn as she started down the hallway.

"Bathroom." She didn't turn back around either and then I heard the door slam shut.

"That's just fucking great," I mumbled to myself. No, fuck that. I marched down to the bathroom and knocked on the door. "We're talking."

"So, talk."

"I want to see your face when we talk."

"I can't look at your face, Rand." Wait—was she crying?

I knocked again. "Open the door, darlin'."

"It's not locked." Brooklyn sniffled.

I turned the handle to find my girl sitting on the counter. I stepped into the room. "Talk to me, Brooklyn," I said softly. "Look at me." I moved close enough to touch her, but I didn't.

Wet tears covered Brooklyn's face when she finally met my eyes. "Tell me the truth, Rand."

"I **never** touched her. I never put my dick inside that woman, and you know it." I cupped her face in my hand. "You broke up with me because you were pregnant, didn't you? Because you thought I would do it first?"

Brooklyn leaned into my hand as she closed her eyes. "I made a mistake."

I brushed my lips against Brooklyn's and my whole body felt like it was on fire. What was it about this woman that made me feel like this? Her hands came up to grab my shirt and she pulled me closer as her tongue slipped inside my mouth.

"Rand." My name on her lips. Fuck, it was so hot and it

made my dick so fucking hard.

Before I knew it, Brooklyn's dress was bunched up around her waist while I pushed her panties aside. Her pussy was dripping wet. "Fuck, darlin'." I growled into her mouth as I let my fingers slip through her damp folds. My dick grew hard as steel.

"Rand, oh, fuck." Brooklyn arched her hips toward me. "More, I need more." She moaned and dug her nails into my chest as she clung to my dress shirt.

I continued to tease her swollen clit as my tongue swirled around her mouth. The sounds Brooklyn made only egged me on. I wanted to impale her on my cock and fuck her senseless. Fuck, I was so hard it hurt. I kissed my way down her neck. Sucked it, licked and left red marks as I continued to play with her little nub.

"Please, fuck me," Brooklyn cried out when I slipped two fingers inside her clenched pussy. "Oh, God!" She grabbed my dick and squeezed it.

"Fuck," I growled as she started to stroke me through my dress pants. "Darlin', you want me that bad?" I pushed against her hand.

"You, Rand. You're who I need."

That was all I needed to hear. I reached over her head to grab a condom out of the medicine cabinet before I unzipped my pants and rolled it over my cock. When I met Brooklyn's eyes, they were wide and full of lust. I slipped off her panties and dropped them on the floor. "Spread those legs for me, darlin'." I told her which she did without a second request. Fuck, she was so ready I could see it dripping down her legs. I moved closer and teased the head of my dick against her clit slowly before I started to ease myself inside. Fuck, so perfect. So wet and warm. So tight.

Brooklyn threw her head back and cried out my name. When did she take her tits out? Her nipples were so hard they pointed straight out. I leaned down to take one in my mouth while I slipped an arm around her waist and angled her body so I could get deeper.

I looked up to watch Brooklyn's face and her eyes had gone wide, her mouth open, but no sound was coming out. "You like that, darlin'? Does it feel good?" I grunted as I thrust inside her. Her eyes rolled toward mine before she bucked her hips.

"So. Good." Brooklyn's voice was hardly a whisper, but I heard her.

I would never love a woman as much as I loved Brooklyn. She could break my heart into a million pieces and tell me she didn't want me, but it didn't matter. I wanted her. I was hers. I clasped my hands behind her hips and pulled her closer. "Fuck, darlin'." I groaned as I felt that familiar heat starting up my spine.

Her lips slammed against mine as she wrapped her legs around my waist. "Rand," she moaned. "Come with me, Rand." She nipped and pulled at my bottom lip with her teeth. "You fill me up so damn good, baby." Her body started to shake and tremble as the orgasm hit her.

I met Brooklyn's eyes as I came in a hot heated rush. I filled that condom so much that I was afraid it wouldn't be enough.

That I would need another one before I was done. My whole body was trembling when I finished and I slipped the condom off and tied it before I tossed it in the garbage.

"I haven't been with anyone since you."

I turned to look at Brooklyn. She was still sitting on the counter, her legs spread and her tits still out. "Darlin', I haven't either." I moved closer. "You should cover yourself before I take you again," I teased.

"Is that a bad thing?" Her voice dripped with heat.

I raised my eyebrows at her. "Brooklyn—" I watched as she stood up and turned around.

"Unzip me." When I didn't touch her, Brooklyn turned her head to look at me. "Rand?" I moved the zipper down her back and watched as the dress she had on fell to the ground. She stepped out of it and turned to face me.

"Upstairs," I ordered her. "My room. Now."

***

Once we got upstairs—after the bathroom—I had pushed Brooklyn up against the wall in the hallway and fucked her so hard I thought I would break the damn thing down. Then she got on her knees and gave me the best blowjob I'd ever had— well, since she got me off in the back yard.

We made it into the bedroom and Brooklyn climbed on top of me and rode me reverse cowgirl. Begged me to fill her. Begged me to fuck her. I could never tell her no, no matter how hurt or upset I was with her. I was still madly in love with her and always would be.

"I should have told you." Brooklyn was sitting cross-legged

on my bed with her dark hair a tangled mess wearing my dress shirt. She looked down at her hands. "RJ knows all about his daddy. I made sure of that."

I had a son. Holy shit. His name was Rand. Brooklyn named him after me. He was the most beautiful thing I had ever seen in my life. I made her show me every single picture she had. Then I made her log into her Facebook and show me those, too.

I was a dad. I was *someone's* dad.

I reached for Brooklyn's hand. "I want to meet him." She tried to pull her hand away. "Stop fighting this, darlin'. What did you think was going to happen? Why won't you look at me? Do you hate me that much?"

"I don't hate you."

My heart caught in my throat when Brooklyn finally looked up at me from under her lashes. It was like the first time I saw her in New Hampshire. The world stopped and my heart started beating so damn fast I thought I was going to die if I didn't touch her or kiss her. Instead, I had acted like my usual asshole self. I reached up to touch Brooklyn's face, but she shook her head.

"Please—I can't," Brooklyn whispered.

"Why? I fucking love you, darlin'. You are everything to me. Why can't you believe that?" I wanted to grab her and kiss her until she couldn't see straight. I wanted Brooklyn to understand that without her? My life was worthless.

Wet tears coated Brooklyn's perfect face. "I ruined everything." A sob escaped her lips. "I shouldn't... I can't... why would you?" She burst into tears.

I was still angry with her for what she did, but I realized that Brooklyn's heart was just as broken as mine was. We could repair our relationship if we both wanted to. I moved closer and gathered my girl into my arms. This time she didn't fight me. I held Brooklyn while she cried. I soothed her by rubbing circles in her hair, my hands cupped against her head as big, angry sobs wracked her small body. I kissed her hair and told Brooklyn how much I loved her. How much I missed her. How I was going to be the best husband and father in the world.

That got her attention.

"What?" Brooklyn blinked at me as tears clung to her lashes. She had makeup smeared all over her face but was still the most beautiful woman in the world to me.

I pressed my lips against her soft, plump ones. "Darlin', it's always been you. It will always be you. Don't you understand that?" I wiped the tears from her cheeks.

Brooklyn sniffed softly before she shook her head. "You're fucking crazy." She attempted to untangle herself from my arms, but I wouldn't let her.

"Tell me you love me."

Heat appeared in her cheeks and for a minute I was afraid Brooklyn was going to deny her feelings. That she was going to try to push me away again. But, she didn't. Instead, she cupped my face with her small hands and smiled at me. "I love you, Rand." Brooklyn's voice shook when she spoke. She took one of her index fingers and slowly traced the bruising around my eyes. "Stop whatever this is. You're only hurting yourself." Brooklyn's finger came down to rub against my lips. "I'm sorry that I hurt you, Rand. That I broke up with you and wouldn't tell you why. I knew you didn't sleep with her." Her brown eyes were wide.

"Come with me." I climbed off the bed with Brooklyn still in my arms. "I want to show you something." I placed her on her feet.

"Do I need to put clothes on?" She grinned up at me and my cock sprang to life. It didn't take much with Brooklyn around.

"No, and I prefer if you stayed in my shirt, darlin'," I teased her. I reached for her hand. I led Brooklyn back downstairs and toward the kitchen. Down the hallway and then I stopped. "Go on."

Brooklyn pushed the door open and gasped. I had the work started right after I told her I wanted her to move in. The studio she would need for her photography. She turned around to look at me. "Rand... this. You did this?" Her chestnut brown eyes were round with surprise.

"I told you I wanted you here with me." I leaned against the door frame. "It's obviously not done, but when you're ready—" I stopped when Brooklyn flung herself at me. She wrapped her arms around me, and I swear she would have climbed me like a tree if I hadn't picked her up. "You like it?" I whispered.

"I love it."

"I've missed you, darlin'. You have no idea what these past three years have been like without you." I pressed my lips against her neck as Brooklyn's legs wrapped around my waist. "You *are* my girl, remember?" I seared my lips to hers and vowed to myself I would never let anything interfere with our relationship again.

Chapter Twenty-Two
SULLY

After we had sex a few more times—I also made sure Rand knew that I was on the pill now, so condoms weren't needed—we ended up in the kitchen where Rand insisted he make me something to eat. Even though it was nearly midnight.

"Sit that sexy ass down and I'll make you something." He winked at me.

"Like what?" I teased as I dragged my teeth across my bottom lip.

Rand growled deep in his chest. "Don't start, or I'll take you right here. Don't you remember what happened when I stayed at your house?" His eyes flashed with heat.

I was glad I put my underwear back on because moisture pooled between my legs. *Again.* "Don't tempt me." I giggled and stifled a yawn.

Rand chuckled. "You sure you don't want to go to bed, darlin'? You look exhausted and I'm sure that—"

He cut off when he heard my phone ringing. "Did I leave my purse in the bathroom?" I bolted off the chair. "Shit." I ran down the hallway toward the sound. Sure enough, there it was. Holy shit, how many missed calls did I have? I was a mom now; I shouldn't be ignoring my phone like that. Just as I started to scroll through, the phone rang again.

"Mia?" I didn't hear anything at first. "I'm sorry I took off from the wedding like that. I'm sure Harper is pissed, but everything is—" I heard crying in the background. "Mia? Is everything alright?"

Rand appeared in the doorway. He had his phone in his hand. Something was wrong and I suddenly felt sick to my stomach. I might have fallen if Rand hadn't been there.

"Mia?" I heard my voice crack. "Look—"

"It's me, Sully." Finn's voice was loud. "Look, I know you and Rand had to work this shit out alone. So that's great." Was he pissed at me? I thought we were over that? "RJ is fine, if that's what you're worried about." He paused and I could hear him talking to Mia. "Your grandparents are going to take care of the twins until Mia can get there."

"What the fuck is going on?" I exclaimed as I stared up into Rand's face.

"It's Aaron."

My stomach dropped. Aaron, Mia's husband, was still stationed in Iraq. "I'm on my way." I hit end on my phone. "I have to leave," I whispered even though I realized Rand already knew. "Can you take me back to Harper's so that I can change? I can't get on a plane dressed in my maid of honor dress." I felt like I was having an out-of-body experience.

"Brooklyn." Rand tucked a finger under my chin. "I'm

sorry." He wrapped his arms around me and pulled me against his chest.

I knew the feeling. The feeling of being told your boyfriend—or husband—wasn't coming home. The dread, the heartache that comes with it. Jesus Christ, Mia must be falling the fuck apart right now.

"I'm coming with you."

I shook my head. "Rand, you don't—"

"Yes, I do. And, I am." He smiled down at me. "I want to meet my son. I want to be there for you, darlin'."

I didn't even try to argue with Rand. He gathered a few items and then we headed back to Lake and Harper's place where I quickly changed so we could get to the airport. I was thankful to have Rand with me. To keep me calm, to talk to me, and to comfort me. Even though it wasn't my husband or my loss, I still knew the grief of what Mia was going through and I knew Rand understood that.

Once we got to Connecticut, Rand had to run to keep up with me. In the airport, in the parking garage to get to my car. I was a lunatic just trying to get home to my friend. To my son.

Our son.

"Don't you think you might want to slow down?" Rand asked as I sped along the highway.

I glanced over at him for a second. "This coming from the man who drives a hundred and eighty miles an hour." I felt his hand on my thigh as he tried to get me to relax.

"That's not on the interstate, darlin', just the racetrack," Rand reminded me. "Ease your foot off the gas a bit before you kill us both."

I knew he was right, so I started to slow the car down. Not to mention the thought of getting a ticket didn't really fly with me either. Rand's hand on my thigh relaxed me a bit, but knowing he would be meeting RJ soon had me all sorts of crazy. This wasn't the way I thought it would happen. I shouldn't have kept this secret from Rand and now I was having second thoughts about everything.

"I know you're worried about your friend. I know the two of you are very close." Rand ran his hand through his thick hair.

I bit back tears. "Rand, she doesn't deserve this. Mia is a good person. She takes care of RJ when I'm working or just because her twins are best friends with him. Those three are tight, you know? Like the musketeers." A small sob escaped my throat. "I just... I wish this wasn't happening right now." I slowed the car and eased off the highway at my exit. "I kept having these memories—" I stopped when I realized what I was about to say.

"Darlin', you can talk about Cooper. You had someone before me, but I'll be the one you're going to marry. The one you spend the rest of your life with," Rand said softly. He might say one thing, but his voice told me otherwise.

Luckily my house came into view, and I pulled into my car into the driveway. It felt like decades since the last time Rand was here. When he came to my house and stole my heart so easily. He was a boy then, but now? Now he was a man. He had grown up over the past couple of years. I could see that now.

"You in there, darlin'?" His hand pressed against my

cheek.

I smiled at him. "Just having a memory. You ready to meet your son?" I asked. Rand nodded his head and turned to open the door. "You don't have to do this if you don't want to." I had seen the look in his eyes. He couldn't hide that from me.

"What if I fuck him up?"

"Rand…"

"I'm serious, darlin'. What if I fuck RJ up like my parents fucked me up? I—" Rand still had his hand on the door.

I climbed over the console and into his lap before I could stop myself. "Rand Shepard." I cupped his face in my small hands. "You are not your parents. You're a wonderful, caring person." His eyes softened when they met mine, but there were tears on Rand's cheeks. "You pretend to be this big, tough-assed man, but I know you. You're going to be the best dad in the world to our son."

Rand's lips tipped up slightly. "I wanted a son, you know?" He brushed his thumb across my bottom lip. "You gave me that, Brooklyn."

My stomach fluttered lightly. "What do you say, you want to come meet him?" I still had my hands against his cheeks and as I went to pull them away, Rand grabbed my wrists. I had never loved someone so damn much. I would spend forever trying to get him to forgive me.

"You're sure?"

I pressed my lips against his before he could say another word and when Rand's hand slipped behind my head, I let out a small sigh. How could I ever doubt him? Why did I do this to him? After making him promise me he wouldn't hurt me or make a fool out of me, I did just that to Rand. I broke his heart.

"I think I'm ready now." Rand's eyes met mine in the dark.

I nodded as I reached for the door to climb out. "My grandparents are here," I warned him. "They were watching RJ and the twins while we—Mia and myself—were gone. So, I guess you get to meet them tomorrow."

Rand didn't say anything as we headed inside the house. It was quiet as we slipped inside. It was after three in the morning, so of course no one would be awake. I knew Rand was worried, but he didn't have to be. I made sure that RJ knew who his father was. He would see that the second we went into his room.

I started to open the door, but when I turned to look up at Rand, he shook his head. His eyes were wide with fright. I was going in anyway. I missed my son. I pushed the door open and stepped into the room.

RJ was fast asleep in his crib while his little nightlight danced around the darkened room. His entire room was decorated in a NASCAR theme. Photos of his father's car were everywhere. He had NASCAR pajamas on at the moment and I reached over to pull the shirt down so that his little stomach wasn't exposed. RJ always looked so peaceful when he was sleeping—not running around like a little maniac or getting into trouble. Not that he did that a lot, but kids were kids. I brushed the dark hair from his forehead as I leaned down to kiss his cheek and breathe in his scent.

"He's so small." Rand's eyes were round with wonder as he watched his son for the first time, and when he met my eyes, I saw love mixed with happiness.

I nodded. "He's tall for his age," I whispered and felt a smile on my lips. "I wonder where he gets that from." I watched as Rand reached down like he was going to touch RJ, but then pulled his hand back. "You can touch him, baby. He's not going to break."

Rand shook his head as he took a step back. "I-I don't—"

I moved around the bed so that I could wrap my arms around my giant of a man. I didn't say anything and then I felt Rand relax before he finally put his arms around me. I would have a few choice words for his parents if I ever had the pleasure of meeting them.

"Let's try to get some sleep." I rested my head on Rand's chest as I looked up at him. "RJ will be up early in the morning and he'll have a million questions for you."

Rand nodded. "Alright, darlin'." His eyes moved past me to where our son was sleeping peacefully in his crib. He looked like he might say something else, but then his focus was on me again.

We slipped out of the room and across the hallway to my bedroom. My grandparents were in the guestroom, but I wasn't worried about waking them up at the moment. I turned around to face Rand who still had a look of fright on his face. I opened my dresser to find a clean pair of pajamas as I waited for him to speak.

"Does—" Rand stopped and I heard him take a deep breath. "Do your grandparents know who I am?"

Was he fucking kidding? Did he think that I wouldn't tell

them who the father of my son was? "Rand, why would you ask me something like that?" I dropped my shirt and bra on the floor before I pulled my tank top on. Then I kicked my jeans off and put my hands on my hips when I turned to face him again.

"I love how sexy you look when you're angry." Rand grinned at me. "Not to mention how you're just standing in your underwear." He grabbed my elbow and pulled me against his chest. "I wanted to make sure I didn't have to explain to them who I was when I asked them if I could marry you."

"What...?"

I didn't have time to say anything else before Rand's lips were on mine and I lost all train of thought. He seemed to do that to me all the time. The way his tongue curled inside my mouth and caused me to moan softly as I leaned into his kiss. I loved him. I fucking loved him with all I had.

"You heard me, darlin'." Rand's voice was soft, his accent thick. "You're mine. You've been mine since the day we met." He cupped my cheek with his hand. "Now let's get some sleep so I can meet our son in the morning." His eyes still looked nervous when he said that last part, but I think he was getting used to it.

I wasn't sure when I finally fell asleep, but it felt like a long time before I finally did. I wasn't the one that was nervous or at least I didn't think that I was. Rand fell asleep the second his head hit the pillow, but I was wide awake.

I knew RJ was going to be excited about meeting his father. He loved Rand even without knowing him. He loved racing, probably as much as Rand did. He wanted to be just like his father. I guess I was worried about that part. Or that Rand was going to have a hard time with how much RJ already looked up to him.

I knew it would work out. It had to work out. I wanted to spend the rest of my life with both of them.

<u>Chapter Twenty-Three</u>
SULLY

I woke up to the sound of my cell phone buzzing and I groaned as I pulled the pillow over my head. I was so exhausted and felt like I hadn't slept at all last night. I was worried about Rand and RJ. My grandparents. Poor Mia and the twins. I reached over to the left for Rand, only to find myself alone in the bed.

Where was he? I sat up only to hear laughing coming from outside the window. I climbed off the bed to pull the curtain back and found my son splashing around in his kiddie pool. With his father. My heart felt like it was going to burst from my chest at the sight as my hand flew up to my mouth. It was such an amazing sight to watch the two of them together.

Rand was soaking wet from head to toe with the biggest smile on his face as he played with his son. It was such a huge mistake to keep them from one another. I never should have kept RJ from his father. Or Rand from his son. I felt like the biggest jerk on the planet. What kind of person does that?

Then my cell phone buzzed again.

I reached for my phone to find that I had several missed calls and texts from Finn. I hope he realized that I had left North Carolina and that I had gone home. I *had* to come home. For Mia. I knew that she was going to need all the support in the world right now and I was surprised that Finn didn't understand that.

Where the hell are you, Sully?

Come on, Sully! Where are you?

Seriously. This isn't even funny.

I texted him back and the second I hit send, he immediately called me.

"Christ, Sully!" Finn exclaimed. "What the hell?"

I looked outside to watch Rand and RJ together. "Finn, you didn't think I was going to stay there, did you? I had to come home. I'm surprised that you're—"

"Of course I know you're home. You could have at least told me! I was worried about you. I could have flown home with you." Finn sounded scared more than upset.

I sighed. "Finn, I'm sorry. I figured you would just come to the house like normal." I suddenly had the urge to be with my son and boyfriend. I needed to hug them. Hold them. Be close to them.

"Sully?"

"I'm sorry, Finn. I'm just..."

"*He's* with you, isn't he? Christ, of course." Finn's voice sounded hurt. Really? This wasn't something new. He was well aware of how I felt about Rand.

"Finn." I turned away from the window. "I love Rand.

We're meant to be together and I'm sorry that you—" I stopped as I tried to get myself together. "I'm sorry that I don't feel that way about you. You're one of my best friends, Finn, but you're going to have to come to terms with the fact that Rand and I are forever. I don't want to hurt you or upset you." I turned back to look outside to watch as Rand picked up our son to swing him around. RJ laughed hysterically before he demanded more.

"I'm happy for you, Sully." Finn disconnected the call before I could say anything else. He was acting really fucking strange. I *knew* he wasn't Rand's biggest fan, but to just hang up on me like that? I thought that we had moved past that shit by now. I went to hit call back on the phone, but decided against it. I didn't want to argue or fight today. Instead, I moved out of the room and started down the hallway wondering if I should call Mia first or wait until a little later. I knew either way she would be slammed with guests.

"Good morning, sweetheart," Papa called to me from the kitchen where he sat drinking his morning coffee.

Here we go. My grandfather had never been a fan of Cooper's. He liked Finn well enough, but had fought me tooth and nail when I told him I was going to marry Cooper. That I had plans to move to North Carolina. He had never trusted him one bit. When he had died, he had been supportive and caring, but I knew deep down he was thankful he didn't have to worry about me leaving. Which I know sounds terrible, but it was the truth.

Now I was going to have to go through all of that again.

I kissed his cheek as I walked into the room. "Morning,

Papa." I noticed that Nana was whipping up what looked like pancakes in her mixing bowl. Interesting. "Good morning, Nana." I smiled at her when she turned to face me.

"Good morning, dear." She winked at me when our eyes met. "That handsome man of yours seems to be enjoying himself." She added as she started to pour the batter into the pan.

"Are you—? What's going on?" I put my hands on my hips. "You met Rand, right?" Not that I didn't want everyone to get along, but this wasn't what I expected.

"We did." Papa stood up and moved over to the coffeemaker. "Nice young man." He dumped a packet of sugar into the cup before he took a sip.

I raised my eyebrows. "You like him? You hated Cooper, Papa," I reminded him. "Don't get me wrong, I want you to like Rand. I love him and I want you to all get along, but I just thought—"

"You thought what, honey?" Papa smiled at me. "Rand is not Cooper. It's obvious how much that boy loves you when he talks about you." He stopped to look out the window before he turned back to face me again. "He asked me if it would be okay to marry you. Did you know he was going to do that?"

I felt myself start to blush. "I...I didn't think he was going to do that first thing." I guess he was really serious. "I love him. I never should have pushed him or kept Rand away from RJ like that. It was wrong. I'm a terrible person."

"You're not a terrible person, darlin'."

I spun around to find Rand standing in the doorway

holding RJ. "How long have you been standing there?" I felt so embarrassed.

"Mama!" RJ wiggled in his father's arms to get down and as soon as he was on the floor, he hurled himself at me so that he could wrap his little body around my leg. "Daddy's here," he whispered as he looked up at me with eyes that matched Rand's.

"Why don't you two go talk for a second?" Nana put her hand on the top of RJ's head as she looked at me. "Nana's making pancakes," she added.

"Pancakes!" RJ exclaimed before he let go of me and moved over to his great-grandmother. The boy could eat like a horse and I knew *exactly* where he got that from.

Rand reached his hand out to me and we made our way downstairs into the family room. I felt nervous for some reason as I turned to look up at him. He looked happier than I had seen him in a long time. Maybe happier than I had ever seen him.

"Everything alright, darlin'?" Rand's hand came up to cup my cheek. "You don't mind that I talked to your grandparents, do you? Or that I was outside playing with RJ?"

I shook my head. "What? No, I want you to spend all the time in the world with RJ. I just... I wish...I wish I had never broken up with you or kept you from him. You should have been there from the beginning."

"Brooklyn." Rand placed both hands on my shoulders. "I should have gone after you. I shouldn't have let you leave like I did, but you know what? We can't go back in time to change it now. But, you can marry me." He suddenly dropped to one knee.

I wasn't sure I had heard him right. Did he just...?

"I've had this—" He pulled a small box out of the pocket of his pants. "I've had this for a while now, darlin'. Longer than you probably realize, and I should have given it to you the second I bought it. So…" He grabbed my hand. "You can say yes and we'll spend the rest of our lives making up for lost time." He met my eyes as he waited for my answer.

I felt my own eyes fill with tears as I stared down at him. "Rand, get up," I whispered softly. There was nothing I wanted more than to marry this man. I knew that, but the way he was looking at me right now was too much.

He shook his head. "Nope, not until you say yes." Rand's lips turned up into a smile.

The ring he had was so damn beautiful. I didn't deserve this man and yet here he was down on one knee asking me to marry him. Asking me to spend the rest of my life with him.

"Darlin', you're scaring me."

I somehow managed to knock Rand to the floor as I covered his perfect face in kisses. I felt his arms wrap around my waist as a deep laugh escaped from somewhere in his chest and when he flipped me around so that I was on my back and he was above me, I saw the look of fear in his eyes. How could Rand possibly think I'd say no? I cupped his face with my hands. "Yes," I whispered softly.

Rand stared at me for a second as if he didn't hear me and then he broke into the biggest smile I had ever seen on his face. He shook his head as he grabbed my left hand to slip the ring onto my finger. "You scared me there for a second." His voice shook slightly when he spoke. "I thought maybe you weren't going to say yes and I wasn't sure I could handle that."

I slipped my fingers into the loops of his jeans before I pulled him closer. "Don't ever doubt my love for you again, Rand," I whispered before his lips were on mine.

I bit back a moan as Rand's tongue slipped inside my mouth as the kiss grew longer and I felt his cock grow hard against my thigh. Fuck, what I wouldn't give right now to just pull off my clothes and ride him right here on the floor. I felt like it had been too long since he'd been inside me.

"Darlin'." Rand growled into my mouth. "You're killing me right now. With your grandparents and our son upstairs. If you're not careful, I'll take you into your studio so that I can have my way with you." He pressed his lips against my neck and I felt the prick of his teeth against my skin.

"Mama! Daddy! Nana wanted me to tell you the pamakes are ready!" RJ called from the top of the stairs in his little sing-song voice. "Hurry before I eat all of them and I'm hungwy." he added. I could only imagine who told him to say that.

Rand started laughing as he pulled me against him in a tight hug. "He's amazing," he said softly and I could hear the love in his voice.

"We really should go up there before he eats everything. Because he'll try," I warned Rand. "He eats a lot for such a little kid."

"I did, too, at his age."

"I figured," I teased and tried to get away from him, but Rand held onto me tightly.

"We'll have more, right?" Rand tilted my head up to look at

him. "Not that I want to rush you or this or anything, but I missed the pregnancy thing and RJ as a baby. I love him, I do. He's me as a kid and I'm happy. So fucking happy, but..."

"We'll have more," I promised. I should have told Rand, I'd regret that for as long as I lived, but I would give him a house full of babies if that was what he wanted.

"Come on, darlin'." Rand squeezed me lightly. "Let's go get some breakfast and then maybe we can spend some time together as a family. Talk about the future and what we're going to do down the line, too. If you want."

I wanted that. I wanted that more than anything.

Chapter Twenty-Four
RAND

I pulled nervously on my tie as I looked around the crowds of people that had come to say goodbye to a man who had served our country. The man was an American hero.

The funeral for Aaron, Mia's husband, was held three days after we returned to Connecticut, and man, I was in awe of how strong my girl was. So fucking strong. Stronger than I was. Of course I tried my damn hardest to block out my feelings and became some sort of stone warrior until she wormed her way into my life. I was fine with that though. She made me want to be a better man.

But, shit. Watching Brooklyn with Mia, comforting her friend the way she did? I'm not sure I could ever do something like that. I've never had to lose something or someone that I loved.

Well, maybe my brother. Eli was the only other person I really loved enough to care about and when he dropped out of my life—fuck. This isn't about him.

I tried to be there for Brooklyn. She was hurting for her

friend and the twins. RJ didn't seem to understand what was going on, but he tried to be there for his friends, too. Noah and Noel seemed confused at the funeral home. They were just kids for God's sake. How do you explain to kids that they will never see their daddy again?

Finn had been acting weirder than normal today. He had avoided me and Brooklyn which really pissed me off. He claimed to love her, but instead had been spending all his time with Mia. I knew they were friends, but it came off as a little strange to me. At least Harper was there to give Brooklyn the extra support I couldn't give her since she and Lake weren't taking their honeymoon until after racing season was over.

"How's it feel, man?" Lake sidled up to me after the service as we stood in Brooklyn's back yard for the reception after the funeral.

I raised my eyebrows at him. "What?" I had no idea what he was talking about. Dammit. I loosened my tie again. I had taken off my jacket, but this fucking tie was strangling me. I wasn't built to be a suit and tie kind of man.

He raised the water bottle he had in his hand to his lips and took a drink. "Being a father." Lake shook his head. "Are you alright?"

"This thing is fucking going to be the death of me." I finally pulled the damn tie right off. "I am not a suit and tie kind—" I stopped just as I saw Mason walk into the back yard. With Apple. "That son of a bitch."

Lake turned to see where I was staring. "Mason? I thought you two were best buddies?"

"I'll be right back." I dropped my tie on the chair with my jacket as I headed straight for Mason. I grabbed him by the elbow and dragged him right back into the house. "You better leave now," I hissed at him. "Brooklyn isn't going to be happy if she sees you."

Mason rolled his eyes. "Why? Dude, that thing with London was a one-time thing."

Fucker knew I wasn't talking about London. He was the closest thing I had to a best friend and I knew him better than he knew himself. I didn't want to get into that. It was who he brought here. To Brooklyn's house. At a funeral. "You need to get her out of here," I warned him.

Mason tilted his head. "Are you serious? I thought—"

"Out of here!" I was so pissed I hadn't realized how loud my voice was. I glanced behind my shoulder to make sure I hadn't disturbed anyone only to find Lake and Finn standing in the doorway. "You can come back, just not with her." I clenched my teeth.

Mason's eyes moved behind me before he shrugged his shoulders. Like it wasn't a *big fucking deal*. Seriously? I was going to have some serious words with him at next weekend's race. "Fine. Fine. Whatever." He turned to look at Apple who was staring at me with that look again. "Let's go, babe."

"What? I thought..." She pouted as Mason turned her around.

"**Don't** bring her around my house again either. Or my RV," I reminded him. "Christ," I muttered as I felt a hand on my shoulder. "I'm warning you!"

"You did a good thing."

Was Finn serious right now? Were we fucking buddies all of a sudden after he avoided me all day? When I met his eyes, he looked… he looked different. "What's that?" I asked him as I folded my arms across my chest.

"What you did. For Brooklyn. You're a good man, Rand. I…" Finn stopped for a second as he took a deep breath. "I shouldn't have given you all the crap I gave you before. About dating her and I'm sorry for that. I know that you're going to be a good husband. Better than my brother would have been."

If this had been a cartoon, my eyes would have popped right out of my head. Did I hear Finn correctly? I chuckled softly. "Maybe you could say that again when I get my phone out. Give me a chance to record it for future use," I teased him.

Finn's lips turned up slightly. "Like hell, Shepard. I just thought I'd get it over with now so that at the wedding I don't have to make some stupid speech." He snorted softly. "Let's go back out there before she wonders what happened to the two of us and thinks I'm beating your ass."

Fat chance that would happen, but I let it go. I made a face at Lake as we went out into the hot sun again, but I didn't have time to say anything when RJ came running at me full speed. I grabbed him and swung him around before I tucked him against my chest. "You behaving, buddy?" I tickled his little belly just so I could hear the sound of his laughter in my ear.

"Daddy." RJ's voice was so soft I could hardly hear him. "Are you going to die?"

Christ almighty, I thought as tears filled my eyes. "RJ…

why... shit," I muttered softly as I turned away from Finn and Lake. What was I supposed to say to that? I was a father now, but I wasn't ready to talk to my son about death.

RJ snuggled closer to me. "You said a bad word, Daddy." He cupped my face with his tiny hands. "Noel said you would." His blue eyes were clouded with sadness. "I don't want you to die. You just home and I want to play more. You make Mama happy. She and I both wove you." The way he said love made my heart melt and I watched as two little tears slipped down his little cheeks.

Shit. Shit. Fuck. I moved away from the crowd of people again. I grabbed my jacket and headed inside the house and out the front door. Then I sat down on the front steps with my son in my lap. I didn't say anything at first. I just held him tightly against me.

"Well, everyone dies, buddy." I said softly as I stroked his dark hair. "Someday—*someday*—I *will* die. But, you'll remember me in so many ways. Good ways. How much I loved you and your mom. How much fun we had together. How I took you racing and how I taught you how to drive a car. It will be okay to be sad when I die. I was sad when my grandfather died." That wasn't a lie, I was sad when my grampy died. I loved that old man a lot. "You can be sad as long as you want *or* if you don't want to be sad, you can tell stories to everyone about how much you loved me." I pulled back so I could look down at RJ. "I know it sounds scary, but I don't want you to think about that now. I want you to think about all the good times ahead. Okay?" I wiped the wetness from his face.

RJ sniffled. "Okay, Daddy." He hugged me as tight as his little arms would allow. "You are the best and I'm so glad you're home. Don't go again."

"I'm not planning on it," I assured him. Then he jumped up off my lap and ran back into the house which left me sitting there alone.

"You are the sweetest man in the world, Rand Shepard."

"Were you standing there the entire time, darlin'?"

Brooklyn sat down next to me. "Pretty much. I saw you pick RJ up and then bring him into the house. He looked upset and I wanted to make sure he was alright." She dropped her head onto my shoulder. "Have I told you how much I love you?" She found my hand and laced her fingers with mine.

"I'd love to hear it again," I whispered. Goddamn, how did I get so lucky? I did not deserve this woman.

"Chasing away the demons. Telling our son about death." She looked up at me. "Supplying me with multiple orgasms on a daily basis."

I brushed my lips against hers. "That last part is free of charge, darlin'. The others? Those are because you do the same for me." I grunted low enough so that Brooklyn understood what I was talking about. She saved me from my demons the moment she kissed me, and I wasn't sure she knew that.

"We're coming back with you."

My head whipped around so fast I thought it might roll right off my neck. "Say that again?" I wanted to make sure I heard Brooklyn correctly.

Brooklyn climbed up onto my lap—fuck, I loved when she

did that—and straddled my waist. "RJ and I are coming back to North Carolina with you. If that's o—"

I stopped her by pressing my lips against Brooklyn's plump ones. I didn't need her to ask if it was okay. Or make sure I wanted that. I needed them with me. I needed my fiancée and son to come home. I wanted RJ to see his new room. To come to his first race. I wanted them both to make my house a home.

To chase away the last of my demons.

"Don't have to ask, darlin'." I nipped at her bottom lip as I pulled back to look at her beautiful face. "It's your home, too."

Brooklyn blushed. "Thank you, Rand." Her eyes searched my face before she spoke again. "For being here. For coming back to Connecticut and…" Her voice trailed off as I ran my thumb across her bottom lip. "I'm going to sell my house here."

"Are you sure that's what you want? I don't want to push you. Take as much time as you need. I'm not going anywhere," I assured her.

"I've already contacted someone to come out tomorrow."

I felt a smile spread across my face as I moved down to press my lips against Brooklyn's neck. "You smell so good," I whispered as I took in her scent. "I love you so fucking much." She tunneled her hands through my hair as I held her. I could end up broke and out of a ride tomorrow, I didn't care. I'd have Brooklyn and I'd still have everything.

The sound of a cough came from behind us. "Sorry to break up your lovefest." Finn sounded less annoyed for once. "But… your son has been trying to find you."

RJ squeezed his way in between the two of us. "Daddy,

you're holding Mama like me." He giggled as he wrapped himself around me.

I met Brooklyn's happy eyes as she made room for our son on my lap. "Sometimes Mommy needs to be held, too." I winked at her as she shook her head.

"Sometimes Daddy needs to be tickled, too," Brooklyn added.

"What? No."

Too late. Both Brooklyn and RJ's hands landed on me before I had time to fight them off—even though I could have—and before I knew it, I was laughing so hard my stomach hurt. I couldn't remember a time I felt this happy and as I managed to get out from under my soon-to-be-wife and son, I felt something hit me. It was fear. Fear that something was going to take this all away from me and I would be left with nothing.

"Rand?" Brooklyn's smile faltered slightly, she saw something in my face. She knew me too well.

"Revenge is sweet, darlin'." I wiggled my eyebrows. First at her and then at RJ. "You better hide, or the tickle monster is going to get you." I laughed evilly as Brooklyn grabbed our son. She took off running into the front yard.

I pushed the thoughts away—the fearful ones—as I watched Brooklyn say something into RJ's ear before I took off after them. I held my hands out in front of myself like I was Frankenstein which sent off a squeal of laughter from Brooklyn before she started to move farther away from me.

I was happy. I was lucky. Nothing was going to take that away from me. I would make sure of that.

Chapter Twenty-Five
SULLY

It wasn't as hard as I thought it would be to leave Connecticut. My best friend had already been living in North Carolina and I wasn't leaving her. My grandparents were snowbirds—which meant they lived in Florida in the winter—and London? Well, she was in New York finishing up school. Or was supposed to be.

I pretended not to know that she was still messing around with Mason. He was—and never would be—good for her. She was old enough to make her own decisions, but I feared he would break her heart. This would leave me to pick up the pieces and hope it didn't bring her eating disorder back. She hadn't shown a single sign of it in two years.

Leaving Mia was hard. After she lost her husband, she was going to need all the support in the world. Not to mention the fact that her boys—Noel and Noah—were super close with RJ. But, her mother was staying with her now. Plus, Mia had mentioned she was thinking about moving back to her home state of California. I was really going to miss her. We'd gotten extremely close. Good thing we had texting.

Or maybe, just maybe, the reason I wasn't having a hard time leaving was because I would be with Rand. We would be a family. The way we would have been if I hadn't been such a jealous asshole and ruined that.

I let all my clients know that I was leaving. I had a couple of photographer friends that I felt comfortable moving them to and those that didn't want to do that? Well, I refunded them their money because it was the right thing to do.

Rand insisted that I hire a moving company to pack up all my stuff—which now I agree was a great idea—and he also insisted on paying for it. I didn't want to take him up on that. I prided myself on being this strong and independent woman. But, if we were going to do this couple thing correctly, I would have to bend a bit. Which I did.

So now? Here we were. As a family. In North Carolina. In this massive house that I had to admit was fucking amazing. RJ was so excited when he saw the back yard—the size alone was probably four times that of ours—that he ran outside without even checking to see what the rest of the house looked like.

"You feel like you can live here?" Rand wrapped his arms around me and rested his chin on my head as I looked around the room that would become my studio. It was pretty much already done. He told me if I needed anything else to go ahead and do it, he didn't care what the cost was.

I leaned back against him. "As long as you're with me I can live anywhere." I looked up to see that big smile on Rand's face. The one that I knew meant he was happy.

"Have you thought any more about coming to the race this weekend?" Rand moved my body slightly so that he could press his lips against mine. "I'd love to have my family there with me."

"It's a big race."

"So?"

I ran my teeth across my bottom lip. "Everyone… people will know I didn't tell you about our son. What will they say?" I didn't want that for Rand. People talking about him like that.

Rand turned me around so that I was facing him. "I don't give a *flying fuck* what people say or what they think. Don't you know that about me by now?" He ran the back of his hand over my cheek. "We made an amazing and beautiful child together. We love one another. What does it matter what anyone thinks?"

I couldn't help but smile at him. "Are you sure that you—"

Rand stopped me when he pressed his lips against mine. "I couldn't be more sure, darlin'. So stop worrying." He pulled me against his solid chest again. "RJ is going to flip out when he finds out he's going to a race, isn't he?"

"You have no idea."

"Daddy!" RJ burst into the room at top speed. "Whose house is that in the back yard?"

I felt Rand's arms tighten around me. "Sweetie." I untangled myself from my giant before I turned to face our son. "Why don't we go see your room? I bet it's a lot bigger than the one you had before."

"Really?" RJ's eyes grew wide.

I nodded. "Uh-huh. I bet it's twice as big." I held out my hand. "Come on." I looked up at Rand. "You, too, Daddy." That at least got him to smile at me, despite the fact that his eyes said something completely different.

The three of us made our way upstairs to the room Rand had saved for RJ and the second our little boy saw it? Well, let's just say he was the happiest I had ever seen him. Rand had decorated the entire thing in a race car theme just like back in Connecticut. The room was a lot bigger and back where we had been living before RJ didn't have a race car bed which was something he had been begging me for. "This—this is all mine?" RJ whispered softly.

Rand nodded. "Sure is." He smiled down at his son. "Do you like it?"

"Daddy. I love it!" he exclaimed. He tangled himself around Rand's leg before he jumped into the room. RJ moved around, examining everything.

I wrapped my arm around Rand's waist. "You did a good job even though I have no idea how you managed to get this finished before he got here," I whispered as I leaned into him. "We're going to be very happy here."

Rand's arm slipped around my shoulders. "I certainly hope so, darlin'." He squeezed me lightly. "Now about that "daddy comment," he teased.

"Rand!"

He chuckled softly as RJ started to dig through the toy chest in the corner of his room. "Tonight," he promised before he let go of me to go over to where RJ was. "What did you find in there, buddy?" He grinned at me over his shoulder before he got down on his knees next to our son.

My stomach fluttered with desire at the thought of what Rand might do to me. Excitement and need pulsed through me as well. It had been a while since we had any time alone and I missed it. I actually couldn't wait for tonight. If we didn't fall asleep from exhaustion first.

***

RJ crashed hard after dinner. He insisted he wasn't tired and was up to watching a movie, but about ten minutes in he was out like a light. Rand carried him upstairs to his bedroom and I followed him while he tucked him in. Then he turned around to face me.

Holy crap.

Fire blazed through Rand's eyes as he started to walk toward me. "Brooklyn," he whispered softly as he got closer and then our mouths were locked together as he kissed me so fiercely I was sure I would lose my breath.

"Bedroom," I murmured and I couldn't help but giggle as Rand lifted me up off my feet.

The second the door latched shut behind us, Rand wasted no time. He pushed my shirt up just enough so that he could get to my breasts and began to suck lightly at the tips one at a time. I let out a low moan as I pulled lightly on his hair. My body was his—only his.

I arched my chest forward as sensations rolled through my body that I swear I had never felt before. "Rand," I whimpered as he licked and sucked hard on my nipples. The fury of desire trembled through my body as the ache between my legs started to grow.

"Darlin', you are so fucking beautiful." His hands skimmed down my hips as he tugged my shorts down my legs. "I hope you know I don't plan on waiting to get inside that sweet little pussy of yours." He dropped his lips against my neck.

I closed my eyes as he kissed my skin lightly. "Touch me. Fuck me. Do whatever you want to me, baby," I told him. "I'm yours."

Rand took a step back. "Is that so?" A sly smile slipped up his lips. "I can see how wet you already are for me." He nodded toward my legs. "Go ahead, darlin'. Get on the bed." He started to unzip his pants. I licked my lips as I sat down and watched as his very hard, very thick dick popped out. "You like what you see?" he teased as he wrapped his hand around his shaft.

I nodded. "Yes." I bit my lip as I sat back on the bed. "Very much." I spread my legs slightly as I waited.

Rand climbed up onto the bed and placed both hands on either side of me so that I was pinned down. "I need you." His eyes were so dark they looked almost black as I felt him nudge at my entrance.

I bit back a scream when he took me with a pounding need. I dug my nails into Rand's back and wrapped my legs around his waist as I begged him for more. His mouth captured my moans as we moved together. As he gave me what we both needed.

"Christ, you feel so good," Rand whispered as our tongues swirled together. "I love you. I will always love you."

I felt a raw rippling wave starting to build inside me as I cupped his face in my hands. "I love you, too," I told him.

I felt like a love streaked comet when my orgasm hit me.

Pleasure tore through me as Rand's sweat-soaked body covered mine. His eyes never left mine as he came with me and he held me so close that I thought I just might break in two.

I had never felt so loved before.

I wasn't sure what time it was when I woke up to the sound of breaking wood. I reached for Rand, but he wasn't there and that's when I realized the noise was coming from outside. I sat up as I listened to what was going on.

Snap. "Stupid fucking asshole." Crash. "I can't believe I was so dumb to think you would get clean and come live here." Thud. "Idiot. I'm an idiot."

What the hell?

When I looked outside, Rand was literally taking apart the house he had built for his brother, Eli. Apart, piece by piece. I grabbed my shirt and shorts off the floor before I checked on RJ to make sure he was alright. I took the baby monitor with me and then headed outside.

"Fucking idiot!"

I skidded to a stop close enough so that Rand could hear me. "Baby, what are you doing?" I tried to keep my voice as calm as possible.

Rand turned around to face me. "Go back to sleep, darlin'. I didn't mean to wake you. This doesn't concern you." He yanked down another piece of wood with his bare hands. That couldn't be good for someone who drove a car for a living.

"It does."

Rand stopped. "I should have done this a long time ago." He hung his head. "Eli isn't coming back here and if he did? I wouldn't let him stay here. He's not—he's not—" He dropped the wood in his hand before he turned to face me. Tears glistened on his cheeks under the moonlight and it nearly broke my heart.

"Baby, talk to me," I pressed him. "I'm here." I moved close enough so that I could touch him. "Rand, I'm here for you," I whispered into the dark as I reached for his hand.

He shook his head. "I never should have had this damn thing built." He laced his fingers through mine. "I never—" His voice caught in his throat as he turned to look at the little house before he finally met my eyes. "I should have burned it to the ground." Rand dropped to his knees. "I don't understand what the hell you see in me, darlin', but if you weren't here..." He let his voice trail off.

I got down onto the grass with him. "Rand Shepard." I cupped his face with my hands so that he had to look at me. "Why can't you understand how amazing you are? What you built here? For your brother? You did a good thing for him because you love him. You're an amazing man even if you don't think so." I kissed his nose lightly. "You put together that room for RJ because you knew how happy it would make him. Because you love him." This time I kissed Rand's forehead. "My studio? You built me an entire studio before we even got back together. Why? Because you loved me." I brushed my lips against his.

"You're my family."

I nodded. "Yes, but if Eli walked through that front door—"

"Fuck him. He's dead to me." Rand's eyes flashed with hate.

"Is he?" I raised my eyebrows as I searched his face. "Baby, I don't think that's true." I slipped my arms up around his neck.

Rand opened his mouth as a storm of emotions rolled across his face. Then he buried his face in my neck and began to cry. Angry, loud sobs escaped his body as he let it all out. My heart ached for him—the man I loved—but I knew that Rand needed this more than he realized. He clung to me so tightly that at times it almost hurt, but I let him let go of his sorrow. Of his grief. The guilt that I knew he carried over not being able to help his brother.

"Fuck." Rand shook his head as he pulled away from me and ran his hands over his face. "Christ, darlin'. It's late. You should go back to bed."

"Are you coming inside with me?"

Rand's eyes were swollen as he looked at me, and I saw the sadness that still weighed heavily on him. He moved fast—like he always did—to gather me into his arms before he swept into me with an earth-shattering kiss. "I don't deserve you," he whispered as he stood up with me still in his arms.

"You do," I assured him. "I wish you realized that, Rand."

He smiled at me as he carried me inside the house and placed me on the bed. I watched as he stripped off his dirty shirt and jeans. "I'm going to take a shower. Do you want to join me, darlin'?" Rand held out his hand.

I giggled softly. "Do you think I'd pass up an opportunity to see you wet and naked?" I made sure that I had the baby monitor with me if RJ woke up—which I doubted he would—before I followed Rand into the bathroom.

Chapter Twenty-Six
RAND

I felt like a complete asshole the next morning when I woke up. I couldn't explain what had come over me last night when I decided to go outside and start tearing the tiny house apart that I had built for Eli.

I guess maybe because I was angry. Hurt. Fucking pissed the hell off? I don't know. I knew that I needed to deal with that anger, too, but I wasn't going to talk to someone about it. Don't get me wrong—that was fine for some people—it just wasn't *my* thing. I wasn't going to go and talk to some stranger about my issues. Those were my personal problems and the only person I had ever told them to was Brooklyn. The fact that she still wanted to be with me was something I couldn't understand, but we worked. We worked damn well together.

"Rand?"

The sound of Brooklyn's voice brought me back to reality as I placed one of the hand weights down that I had been lifting. "In here, darlin'," I called to her. I had this gym built with the house and I never used it. I guess now was a good time to start.

"What are you—oh." She stopped in the doorway as she looked around the room. "Did you sleep at all last night?" Brooklyn's brown eyes were wide as she stepped into the room.

"Some." I wiped the sweat from my forehead. I noticed the way Brooklyn was watching me and I couldn't help but chuckle. "You like watching me like this? All sweaty?" Her cheeks turned pink. "Come here, darlin'." I crooked my finger at her.

Brooklyn giggled as she did as I asked. "This is—" She stopped when I pressed my mouth against hers and she slipped her tongue between my lips without hesitation.

"Where's RJ?" I whispered as I pulled back to look at her.

"Outside with Lake and Harper."

My eyebrows went up. "Lake and Harper are here?" I wasn't used to people just stopping by, but I guess I was going to have to get used to that now. The whole having friends come over thing. I had Mason, but that was different. He wasn't someone I felt comfortable just hanging around with. We drank. We picked up girls—okay, he picked up girls now—but we used to pick them up together and that was it. I wasn't even sure he knew how to be someone's friend. I was trying to learn that, too. I still wasn't sure why Lake asked me to be in his wedding and I only did it because I knew Brooklyn would be there.

Brooklyn nodded. "They just wanted to see how I was settling in." She stood up on her toes and kissed my chin.

I cupped her face with my hands before I dropped another kiss against her soft mouth. "How *are* you settling in, darlin'?" I slowly ran my tongue across her lips.

Brooklyn's cheeks turned pink again. I loved how she got

easily embarrassed about sex. Even now. "Do you want me to tell them I'm settling in just fine and fucking my fiancé as often as I can?"

I dropped my hands so that I could cup her round ass before I pulled Brooklyn against me. Right up against my hard dick. "That sounds about right to me." I growled deep inside my chest.

"Are you two about done?"

I looked up to find Harper standing in the doorway. Sure. Okay. Just make yourself at home. In my house. I knew she was Brooklyn's best friend and married to my friend, but really? I still didn't think she liked me.

Brooklyn buried her face against my chest as she giggled nervously. "Harp, maybe you could, I don't know? Knock or something next time?" She clung to my shirt as she tried to turn to look over her shoulder.

Harper broke into a grin. "Sure. Next time." She folded her arms across her ample chest and if I was a betting man, I might have noticed a small baby bump underneath her dress. Was she pregnant?

My brain flashed back to the day Lake asked me what it felt like to be a father—was that what he was getting at? Was he trying to hint about Harper being pregnant? Did Brooklyn know? Maybe I should let them have some sort of girl time.

"You two all set in here or what?"

I nodded. "Sure, I just need to change. Tell Lake I'll be out in a second." I managed to grab Brooklyn before she followed her friend outside. "I love you," I said softly. "Go on, darlin'.

Spend some time with your friend. I just want to change my shirt."

"Are you alright? About last night..."

I shook my head. "I'm going to be fine, darlin'," I assured her. "I promise. If I need to talk about it, you will be the first person I come to."

I would be fine. I would make sure of that.

***

Hanging out with the Mills—that sounded fucking weird to me—wasn't as bad as I thought. It was kind of awesome to not have a huge party with a bunch of people drinking and getting drunk just to get drunk. Not just hanging out at your house because of who you were. It was just the four of us and RJ.

RJ loved having an audience to goof around with, too. He was a total ham. He was going to love being a driver.

And, yes. Harper was pregnant. I thought that Brooklyn was going to lose her ever-loving mind when Harper told us that day. Her best friend was having a baby. RJ would have a friend to play with. I hoped it would be a boy so that there wouldn't be a girl around. You know what I mean?

That was five days ago and now? Now we were in Indianapolis for the race. As a family.

"Darlin', you about ready to go?" I had practice to get to before I was late. I couldn't be late or else I'd be in some serious trouble. I didn't need that. I was ready to finally turn my shit around after the past couple of years. Starting today. When I didn't hear anything from my fiancée—shit, I loved how that sounded—I moved back into the bedroom. "Brooklyn? What are you doing?"

She was sitting on the bed with her head in her hands. "I can't do this, Rand." She looked up at me. "This—this whole pretend everyone isn't going to care about you suddenly having a kid thing. What are your fans going to say? Your team? Your car owner?" Her face had grown incredibly pale. I knew Brooklyn had been worried, but not this worried.

"Hey." This seemed to be my typical move with Brooklyn and I would do it for her if it meant she would be mine forever. I dropped to my knees in front of her so that we were eye to eye. "Fuck what they think. Haven't we already talked about that?" I let my fingers graze her chin. "My fans will be happy for me, darlin'. They want me to be happy, right?" Brooklyn's lips turned up slightly. "My team knows already. As does Brian." That was my car owner. He knew a lot because he was up my ass sideways these days. Making sure I wasn't getting into any more trouble.

I was lucky I still *had* a fucking ride.

When Brooklyn didn't say anything, I traced her lips with my fingers. "You are my world. Do you understand that? You and RJ. My fucking everything. I'll punch every motherfucker who tries to say otherwise." I brushed my mouth against hers. "I'd die for you, you know that, right?"

"I know that, Rand." Her eyes glistened with tears.

"Daddy, you said a bad word." RJ wiggled his way between us. "You need to put a quarter in the swear jar."

Ha! I'd have to put a lot more than a quarter in the swear jar. I guess I would have to learn to keep my swearing down, too. "Okay, buddy. I can do that." I ruffled his hair. "Is this family going racing or what?"

"Yes!" RJ exclaimed. "Right, Mama?" He looked up at his mother with big blue eyes.

Brooklyn smiled at me. "Yes. Of course we are."

As we made our way down to the track, it was obvious people were watching us. Maybe they were shocked that Brooklyn and I were back together. Or that RJ was with us. But the second Harper walked up to us with Lake everyone seemed to find something else to gossip about. They always did. That's sort of what the NASCAR family did. Others would probably still talk about it, but that was what they did. They'd get over it soon enough.

The weekend flew by and maybe I enjoyed myself more than I normally did because I had my family with me. I was happier. More relaxed. I felt like I was more easygoing than normal, too. I hoped that everyone else saw it that way.

I couldn't help but feel a little nervous for the race though. It might have been because Brooklyn had never seen me race before and I wanted to win for her. Or it might have just been me. I just didn't normally get nervous before a race. It was bugging me, and I tried really hard to shake the feeling off.

Also, why was it so damn hot today? I was sweating my damn balls off inside this fire suit.

"Break a leg." Brooklyn giggled as she hugged me right before I had to climb into my car.

I raised my eyebrows. "Really? That's what you're going with?"

"Isn't that what you say to someone to wish them good luck?" She leaned back against the side of the car as she watched me.

"Win, Daddy!" RJ was sitting against my hip already wearing his earplugs, but he gazed up at me with happiness in his eyes. I'd win just for him. I wanted to make him proud of me.

I kissed the top of his head. "I'm going to try my best, buddy."

"We'll be here when you're done," Brooklyn said softly.

I pressed my lips against hers. "I love you, darlin'," I whispered against Brooklyn's ear as I pulled her into a hug.

"I love you," she whispered back.

I handed RJ over to Brooklyn before I climbed into my car, feeling well aware that she was still watching me. I picked up my helmet only to notice that my hands were shaking. Shit. Why were they shaking like this was my first race? For the love of fuck, what was wrong with me today?

"Rand?"

I turned at the sound of her voice. "I love you," I said again and watched her entire face light up. "I know you'll be listening on the radio." I had made plans for Brooklyn and RJ to sit up in my pit box today. They would get a better view of the race and would be able to listen on my radio as well.

"Come on." Harper walked up next to my car. "It's time to get us girls comfortable so our men can do their thing."

"Hey!" I put my hand out the window and Brooklyn took it. I squeezed her hand lightly before I tugged on her hand so that she moved closer. Harper took the hint and lifted RJ from her arms before Brooklyn leaned down into the car. "Kiss me, darlin'. A real kiss."

Brooklyn moistened her lower lip with her tongue before she moved in to press her lips against mine. This wasn't a gentle kiss—it was a kiss that sent my heart racing and woke my dick right the fuck up. The little prick of her teeth as she nibbled on my bottom lip before her tongue found mine was enough to make me nearly pull Brooklyn right into the car with me.

"Alright, break it up." Harper chuckled. "You can do that later."

Brooklyn placed two fingers against my lips. "I love you," she said. "Go kick some major ass, Shepard."

I watched her walk away until I couldn't see her anymore and then I felt better. Much better. Like a giant weight had been lifted off of me. The nerves were gone. The strange feeling that I had earlier was gone, too. I felt more like myself and ready to get out on the track to kick some major ass. Just like Brooklyn had said.

Then I started thinking. What if—and this was a big fucking if—I won this damn thing. For my girl. For my kid. I mean, I would have to make it through four hundred laps and I was starting in the twentieth position, so I wasn't exactly in the best spot. But, it could be done. I would just have to keep myself from getting wrecked and as long as my car was as good as it was in practice—which was pretty damn awesome—I would be golden.

It had been a while since I had won a race. A long goddamn while, but as I started my car and started to roll out onto the track, I realized just how badly I wanted it.

The only problem was that I didn't expect the two rookie drivers in front of me to cause a crash fifty laps in. Bumping and hitting one another like we had two damn laps to go. This was not how you raced this early in.

This was how crashes happened.

This is how you crashed good cars.

This would be how I ended up getting taken out of the race.

Chapter Twenty-Seven
SULLY

Watching Rand's crash was like my worst nightmare.

It wasn't that I didn't know crashes happen in NASCAR because I knew they did. It's how Cooper died and I'd seen them happen on countless other occasions.

Just never in person.

The second I saw someone hit him, I lost it. The moment I saw Rand's car spin around and hit the wall, I started screaming. I screamed so loud that I nearly lost my voice. I screamed so loud and so long that my head hurt like someone had taken a sledgehammer to it.

My only thought was that my fiancé—the man that I loved and wanted to spend the rest of my life with—and the father of my son—was hurt.

Or maybe worse.

I didn't really remember too much after that. I was an absolute lunatic trying to get to Rand. No one seemed to know if they took him to the hospital or if he was just being checked at the infield care center. No one seemed to be able to tell me anything because I wasn't Rand's wife.

"Sully, you need to relax." Harper slipped her arm around my shoulder. "I'll have Lake find out."

I clenched my teeth together. "I. Need. To. Know. *Now*," I hissed at her as my throat burst into pain. I suppose screaming like that hadn't been the best idea. "Rand..."

"I know. I know." Harper nodded. "We're going to find out," she assured me. "Freaking out on everyone isn't going to do you or Rand any good." Her eyes flicked to where RJ clung to me with wide blue eyes. "Hey, sweetie. You want to go see Uncle Lake?"

RJ shook his head just as he popped his thumb into his mouth. He only did that when he was upset or sleeping. I needed to get my shit together for my son.

"Sully."

I turned at the sound of my name to see Finn and before I could stop myself, I fell into his arms. Finn—my comforter and brother. My other best friend. It wasn't that Harper wasn't the support I needed, but Finn was different.

Finn wrapped his arms around both of us just as his hand smoothed down my hair. He and Harper must have been communicating without saying anything because it was quiet. Too quiet.

"What are you not telling me?" I croaked out.

"He's been moved to the hospital."

"What!"

"Brooklyn—" Finn put both his hands on my shoulder as he pulled back to look me in the eyes. "They moved Rand to the hospital, but that's all I know. That's all they will tell me."

I felt sick. I felt like I was going to pass out. I wasn't going to be able to handle this again.

"Don't pass out," Harper warned me. "We'll get there. Come on."

"The traffic, the crowds of people..." Hot tears pricked behind my eyes.

"Helicopter."

My eyebrows shot up as I turned to see Mason standing in the doorway. "Excuse me?" My voice was a hoarse whisper. He was not my favorite person right now; *in fact*, you might say I almost hated him. With him and London messing around, I wanted nothing to do with him. Not to mention the fact that he brought Apple to *my* house.

Yes, I fucking knew about that.

"Look." Mason stepped forward. "I know you don't like me, Brooklyn. That's fine; you don't have to like me. Let me do this for you and RJ. Let me take you to the hospital via helicopter. Right now. We'll get there way fucking faster."

I didn't even bother to correct him about the language. I nodded. "Let's go." I coughed out the last part.

Mason turned to go and I followed him with hesitation with RJ snug against me. I'd deal with my issues with the man later. Right now I had to get to Rand.

***

The hospital was huge. I mean gigantic. Enormous. At least triple the size of anything I had been inside of before. Bigger than anything that London had spent time in. It was also incredibly overwhelming. I bit down on my lip as I slipped inside the building, Mason right behind me.

"Where?" I turned to look at Mason who looked like he might have a little bit of a clue where we needed to go.

Maybe?

"I got this." He nodded before he stepped in front of me. "Excuse me, Annie?" He moved right up to a nurse that had been checking him out. "My friend here is looking for her husband—Rand Shepard? He was in a racing accident earlier—NASCAR—I don't suppose you know where he might be?" He let a slow, sexy smile spread across his handsome face.

Annie turned pink the second Mason said her name. "Oh... well... uh... I really shouldn't do that. Not without making sure you're who you say you are. You know privacy and all." She batted her eyelashes so many times I wanted to throw up.

"Mama? Where's Daddy?" RJ blurted out.

"Sweetheart, we're going to see him soon." I kissed his forehead. "I promise."

Mason leaned against the counter. "My nephew here? He's really upset about his father, too. I understand you have rules and HIPPA. Totally get that." He placed his hand flat down on the counter. "But, maybe this one time?" Damn, he was good at this flirting thing. I'd give him that much. Maybe that's why London had jumped into bed with him so fast.

Fucking gross.

Again Annie looked between the two of us before she spoke. "Come with me." She jutted her chin toward a set of locked doors and in a second was walking toward them. She swiped a card and boom—we were in.

Shit. Crap. Motherfucker.

"I told you." Mason winked at me. "I'm good at—"

"Don't you dare," I warned him. "I still don't like you," I reminded him.

Mason nodded. "Good to know, Brooklyn." I noticed the hurt in his eyes, but I didn't care. He had to know why. Although maybe I hated him a little less right now.

"I didn't let you in," Annie whispered as she stopped in front of a room. "I better get something out of this, Mason Pelletier." She locked eyes with him before she hightailed it away from us.

"Ladies first." Mason motioned for me to go into the room.

I shook my head.

"Brooklyn."

"Mason."

Mason took a step toward me. "Look." He ran his hand through his hair. "Go in there and see your boyfriend. The man needs you right now. I've never seen him like this when it comes to a woman—*ever*. He fucking loves you. Cooper? He wasn't right for you. I'm sorry to say that, but it's the truth. But, Rand? Rand is your soul mate. Your one true love. That happily ever after shit isn't in the cards for me, but it is for him. He's the one person you were meant to be with. Get in there before I carry you inside the damn room." His nostrils flared angrily at me.

My hatred might have changed to dislike right there.

"Uncle Mason, you need to put a quarter in the jar," RJ called out to him as I pushed the door open. I'd correct him on the Uncle part later.

I hated hospitals. The smells and the sounds. I just—they were too much for me.

Rand was lying on a hospital bed with his eyes closed. There were a few machines hooked up to him, but they didn't look *too* serious. At least, not that I thought. I had seen horrible and serious machines before. London had been near death a couple of times with her eating disorder. Feeding pumps. Feeding tubes. That sort of thing.

Rand's right leg was in a cast while his face looked pretty bruised. Again. His left arm was in a sling and his breathing was pretty relaxed. I figured that he was probably on some serious medication right now. When he woke up he might be in a lot of pain.

"Mama," RJ whispered into my ear. "Is Daddy sleeping?"

I nodded my head as I swallowed back the tears that threatened to fall. He was alive. That was the important part. I held my finger up to my lips as I moved closer. I just, I just needed to touch him. Make sure he was real.

I placed RJ onto the floor as I approached the bed and I did what I knew Rand would do. I got onto my knees. "I'm sorry." My voice cracked as I spoke the words. "I wish it was me. I wish I could change places with you, Rand. You don't deserve this." I dropped my forehead against the mattress and—again—fought the tears.

"I wouldn't be able to handle it if this was you, darlin'. Besides, I just broke a leg, an arm and fractured a couple of ribs.

I'm going to live."

My head shot up so fast I nearly fell over. Rand was awake and staring at me with that damn sexy smile on his face.

"Right here." Rand moved his hand up to his lips. "Give me a kiss before I die," he teased me.

I climbed up onto the bed and slammed my lips against his. "Don't you dare do that again, Rand Shepard."

"Daddy!" RJ exclaimed as he realized his father was awake. Then he, too, was climbing up in the bed. Good thing Rand was such a giant and they had given him an extra-large hospital bed told hold all of us.

"How did you get here so fast?" Rand looked exhausted and I knew we wouldn't be able to stay long. As soon as the doctors and nurses realized we were there? We were screwed.

"Mason."

Rand's eyes went wide. "What happened to your voice? And, Mason?" He pressed his lips against mine again. "The helicopter." He didn't ask that part, it was more of a statement. "You let Mason fly you in his helicopter?"

"Yes." I snuggled closer to him to try to take in his scent. "I lost my voice when you crashed, Rand. I sort of freaked out."

Rand didn't say anything right away and for a minute I thought he fell asleep. "Marry me," he whispered.

"Rand, didn't we already go over that part?"

"Tomorrow. Right here. We'll get the chaplain to marry us."

"Are you serious?" I sat up to look at his face. He was dead fucking serious. "Yes."

Rand broke into a smile. "Call Harper. Get her ass here so

she doesn't kill me for you getting married without her. Get your sister here, too. Get whoever else you want."

"What... who... who do you want as your best man?" My brain was already thinking about Mason. He got me here. I didn't even ask.

"I don't care." He had closed his eyes again.

"What about Mason?" I chewed on my lip as I watched his eyes pop back open. "He-he did me a big favor, Rand. He..."

"I'd like it to be Mason. He's one of my closest friends." He smiled at me. "Goddamn, I love you."

"I'll go call Harper and London. I'm sure it will take a little while, but she'll be here. Get some rest, baby." I kissed him again before I climbed off the bed. "I love you, too" I added before I picked RJ back up.

"Not as much as I love you, darlin'." His voice sounded like he was already falling back to sleep.

I shut the door behind me and made my way out into the waiting room. Finn, Mason, Harper, and Lake were there. I smiled at them as I moved into the room.

"Well?" Harper was first on her feet.

"He's going to live. He has a broken arm and leg, but he'll be okay."

The entire waiting room exploded into excitement and I couldn't help the smile that grew bigger across my face. "Guys, guys! I have to ask you a few things." I looked at Mason first. "Will you be Rand's best man?"

"What?"

"We're going to get married. As soon as we can. *Here*. He

wants you to be his best man. I want you to be his best man. After everything you did today." I moved closer so that I could hug him. "Please?"

Mason hugged me back but looked confused. "Sure, but...?"

"No buts." I shook my head. "Harp? You're my maid of honor. I have to call London. Oh—Mia! Maybe I can get her here, too. I wonder if she could get here tomorrow."

"You need a dress!" Harper exclaimed.

"I don't..."

"You do. We'll get you one. Something beautiful, but something that is *you*." Finn smiled at me.

"Finn." I felt my eyes fill with tears. "Will you give me away?"

"Sully, I would be honored." He nodded his head.

I bit my lip. This is happening so damn fast, but it was what I wanted. I loved Rand so much and couldn't imagine being without him. Or being with anyone else.

Not ever.

"Sully?"

I looked over at Harper who was watching me. "Let's go get that dress. RJ, you want to stay with Uncle Finn?

RJ nodded just as Finn picked him up. "We'll be here when you get back."

I hugged him again before I turned and rushed out of the hospital with Harper. This was crazy. But I wouldn't have expected anything else with Rand.

Chapter Twenty-Eight
RAND

I wasn't fucking around anymore. I was going to marry this fucking woman and that was that. No one was going to stop me. Not even my doctor.

"Mr. Shepard..."

"Sorry, doc." I shook my head. "I know you don't think it's the best idea for me to get out of bed yet, but I'm getting hitched." I was sitting up now at least. The wedding was scheduled to be today—which was about twenty hours after my accident—and I could hardly stand it.

Fuck no, I wasn't nervous. I was excited and couldn't wait to call Brooklyn my wife. She'd be Brooklyn Shepard after today. She had better be planning on taking my last name, too, because there would be one hell of a big argument if she didn't.

Dr. Harrison sighed. "You can't wait a week? This woman—"

"Is the one, doc." I looked up as Mason and Lake walked into the room. Mason was carrying a garment bag which I assumed contained my suit. I had given him my measurements after he asked me.

Dr. Harrison sighed. "Fine." He glanced at my friends before he looked over at me again. "No sex. Those ribs need to heal." He smirked at me before he leaned closer. "Maybe a little quickie, but then I want you back in this bed. Eat all the cake you want with your new bride."

I grinned at him. "Thanks, doc." I felt my heart swell with happiness. Cake I couldn't care less about, but I wanted to get better as soon as possible so that I could get back to work. Get back to my almost wife and son.

"You getting cold feet yet?" Mason teased me the second the doctor was gone.

"Fuck off," I told him. "That had better fit, asshole, or you're going out to get another one."

Mason laughed before he made himself comfortable in one of the chairs in the room. "Relax, gigantor. It's going to fit."

Lake snickered. "Remember this when it's your turn." He pointed a finger at Mason. "We're going to give it to you ten times worse."

"The fuck you will. I'm a bachelor for life and you assholes know that." Mason had a horrified look on his face.

"That so?" Lake leaned back against the wall as he folded his arms across his chest. "So you're just going to pork every pit bunny that comes along until you retire and then what? Just pick up chicks in bars? Settle with the rotten fruit girl?"

"Apple is not who I want to settle down with *if* I was going to settle with someone." Mason rolled his eyes.

"London maybe?" I wiggled my eyebrows. "Don't think we

all don't know you were banging Brooklyn's sister. Don't think *she* doesn't know either."

"It was ONE time at Lake's damn wedding! She came after me and only after I tried to turn her down—" When Lake and I both started laughing, Mason stood up. "You know what? Fuck you both. I'll see you at the wedding."

"Dude! We were just kidding!" I called out to him, but he just flipped me his middle finger without even looking back. That only made us start laughing again. I guess we're kind of assholes, but honestly? He had it coming. Guy was worse than I was when it came to women.

Lake shook his head as he moved into the seat Mason just got up from. "Pretty sure he's in love with her."

I stared at him. "Say that again?" Brooklyn was not going to want to hear that.

"London. Mason's in love with her. He doesn't really understand the feeling, but I know the look. You had it when you first met Brooklyn. I had it when I first met Harper." Lake shrugged. "We all come from fucked up lives. We don't understand what that feeling feels like…"

"Mason is not in love with London. Brooklyn will kill him," I insisted, but the more I thought about it? The more it started to make sense. He had been acting weirder than normal lately. Shit.

Lake tipped his head back and laughed. "Sully isn't going to be able to control it, Shepard. She fell for you, didn't she?"

"Ass." I threw my pillow at him, but he caught it and threw it back at me.

"Everything alright in here?" Finn knocked lightly at the door. "You're looking better than I thought." He nodded at me.

Was that a compliment? I wasn't so sure. I couldn't figure out if Finn actually still hated me or not. We would never be best friends, but maybe we could manage to have a civil conversation once in a while. "Thanks." I nodded back at him. "How's Brooklyn?" I couldn't wait to see how beautiful she looked. I didn't care if she was wearing a paper bag, she'd rock that shit.

"Excited," Finn told me. "Lake, can I have a minute with Rand?"

What the fresh hell was this?

"Uh, sure." Lake stood up. "I'll see you at the wedding, I guess." He gave me a strange look before he left the room.

"Look." Finn sighed. "You and I haven't always gotten along." He walked over to the window. "I haven't always been that nice to you."

Understatement.

"I haven't always been that nice to you either."

Finn turned back around. "I know you love her. I know you're going to take care of her. You've proven that to me. I know that I can trust you with Brooklyn and that's..." Finn looked up at the ceiling before he looked at me again. "That's hard for me. I've been in love with her since I was fifteen and it's not ever going to happen between us. Cooper hurt her. Over and over again. I couldn't stop that." He took a step closer to me.

"I won't hurt her. I've been in love with Brooklyn since the second I met her." I didn't remind him he introduced us. Salt— wound. That sort of thing.

"She was it for me, man. You know that."

"I know."

"So—"

"This does not mean we're going to be best friends," Finn cut in. "But, you know."

"Sure." I didn't, but that was fine. I'd figure it out later.

Finn looked relieved to have that conversation out of the way. "You hang out with some real assholes." He moved so that he was looking out the window again. "I mean, Lake is alright, but Mason?"

"Mason's not that bad. You just have to get to know him." I wondered how I was going to get dressed with a cast on my leg and a sling on my arm. "Uh, Finn?"

"You need help putting on that suit?" He turned back around. "That can be my gift to you. For the wedding." He looked so damn serious until he broke into a smile. "I'm kidding, man. Relax." He shook his head. "As long as I don't have to see your dick, I'll help you."

I didn't bother to tell him that I didn't have on any underwear. I guess that could be my little wedding gift for him.

I'm still an asshole when I want to be.

** *

Lake managed to wheel me down to the chapel for the wedding because of all the broken bones. It also meant that I wouldn't be standing for Brooklyn as she walked down the aisle but I would still be waiting for when she got there.

"Suit fits?" Mason asked as Lake put on the brakes so I wouldn't accidently roll away.

I was about to give him a snarky answer, but I didn't have time.

I don't know where Brooklyn managed to get that dress on such short notice, but all I could think about was ripping the damn thing off of her. She looked fucking fantastic. It was like the first time I saw her, the world stood fucking still, you know? It fit her perfectly, falling right to her knees with some lace shit all over it. It was sleeveless, but it had straps that went up around her neck.

The woman was a fucking knockout and once again, I wondered how I got so damn lucky.

Brooklyn had her dark curls pulled up onto her head with some white flowers sprinkled in. No veil, but she didn't need a veil. I wanted to see her smiling face when she walked toward me. And? She was smiling so big that it made my heart feel like it was going to burst out of my fucking chest.

I realized that I was smiling like that, too.

"Hi," Brooklyn whispered when she was close enough. She blushed slightly when I took her hands.

I was fucking speechless. "You—" I couldn't even form words right now. I was the luckiest bastard in the world. "You look amazing, darlin'." I watched as she turned even pinker.

Don't ask me about the wedding part because I don't remember. Someone went out and got us gold bands. I think it was Finn. You heard me right—Finn—and they weren't cheap ones either. They were nice as shit and I was going to have to thank him for that.

I guess the bastard really meant what he said.

Then? Well, then we were married. I was someone's husband. Shit, I was Brooklyn's husband. But, the best damn part was that she was my wife. Mine. Forever. I pulled her against me and kissed her. Kissed her plump, soft lips until I was pretty sure neither one of us could breathe anymore. Brooklyn didn't seem to care though because when I tried to pull away, she grabbed my tie to keep me there.

"You're mine now, Shepard." Her brown eyes twinkled with happiness. "My husband."

I felt that stupid smile slip across my face. "That's right, darlin'." I placed my hand against the back of her head fully aware that everyone was watching. "Which means you're my wife."

"Um... if you two are done." Mason coughed loudly. "There's a small reception in the cafeteria."

Brooklyn pulled her eyes away from me. "What?" She sounded surprised.

That makes two of us.

Mason chuckled. "Surprise."

"How... what?" She turned to look around the chapel. "You guys did that?"

RJ rushed up to hug us. He had been silent through the entire ceremony even when he brought the rings up to us, but Brooklyn stopped him before he climbed into my lap.

"You deserve this," Harper spoke up. "You can't have a wedding without a reception."

I guess I really did have friends now.

"Thank you," I said softly. "You all have done so much for

us already." I felt Brooklyn's arm around my waist. "I know I haven't been the nicest guy in the past, but I guess I needed the right woman to come along to change me. To make me realize that life is worth so much more." I meant it, too. "Anyway, let's go eat."

I wanted to go fuck my wife, but that was going to have to wait until later.

"You're something else, Rand," Brooklyn said softly. "I always knew you weren't the guy you tried to be."

"You did that."

Brooklyn shook her head. "You did that. I just helped you open yourself up."

I placed RJ down on the floor so that I could cup her face in my hands. "You're the best thing that has ever happened to me," I whispered. "My whole life has changed because of you."

"And mine because of you." She touched my cheek with her hand. "I love you."

"I love you." I kissed her forehead. "I plan on knocking you up again the first chance I get." I watched as Brooklyn's eyes went round. "Okay, maybe not right away, but I missed out on so much. The big pregnancy belly, the birth of our son. I want to experience everything with you. I love RJ, but wouldn't a little girl make you happy?" I suddenly realized if we had a girl there would be boys sniffing around when she was older. "Shit, maybe another little boy?" I suggested.

"Let's worry about that when the time comes." Brooklyn giggled as she grabbed RJ who came running toward her. Mason started to push me down the aisle and I couldn't help but feel happy.

So fucking happy.

My heart was full and nothing could ruin that.

Chapter Twenty-Nine
SULLY

If you had told me that I would end up married to Rand Shepard, I would have thought you were crazy. But, guess who married Rand Shepard? That's right—that would be me. I married the bad boy. The sexy as all hell, tattooed, giant NASCAR driver. The one who thinks I hung the moon and stars when, in fact, that's how I feel about him. He makes my world a better place just by being in it.

Because before Rand came into my life, I was hardly living, and now? Now I'm the happiest I've ever been.

Alright, enough sappy shit.

Let's just talk about my goddamn dress for a second. This little knit thing with the floral lace overlay and the cami-straps? It was so damn perfect. Only fifty bucks, too. I didn't want a white dress, but Harper thought it was only right I wear white on my wedding day. What she wants, she gets. That's how my best friend works.

I cried when I put it on and then I didn't want to take it off.

The look on Rand's face when he saw me was all I really needed to know that it was the right choice.

He looked fantastic, too. He could stand there in a plastic bag and he'd look good. The man was a fucking Greek god.

"Look at all this," I whispered to Rand as Mason pushed his wheelchair into the hospital cafeteria. Our friends and family had decorated it for us, it was beautiful. There were white balloons and flowers everywhere. I felt my eyes fill with tears as I saw how hard they worked.

"Darlin', I hope those are happy tears." Rand brushed my hair back from my face as he spoke.

I nodded my head. "Trust me when I say they are." I climbed off his lap once Mason had stopped the wheelchair. I noticed Mia in the corner working on the finishing touches of what looked like the most amazing cake I had ever seen and my stomach growled like I hadn't eaten in days. Come to think of it, when was the last time I had eaten a proper meal?

"Hey." Rand tugged on my elbow. "I hope you know when this is all said and done, I'm taking you on a proper honeymoon. When the racing season is over and I'm healed up." He laced his hand through mine.

I shook my head. "You don't have to do that." I moved in closer so that I could drop a kiss against his mouth.

"I know, darlin', but I want to. Can you imagine us sitting on a beach somewhere?" He chuckled softly. "I want to see you in a bikini, the smallest fucking bikini you can find." A growl escaped his chest. "Tell me where you want to go and I'll make it happen."

"Hawaii." I had always dreamed of a honeymoon there, but never thought it would happen.

"Then guess where we're going to go on our honeymoon?"

"Alright you two," Harper interrupted us before Rand could say anything else. "I know that you're newlyweds now and everything, but you need to do a few things before you can go off and.. well... you know." She snickered at herself. "How about you sit down and have something to eat? We've got a shit-ton of food."

"Auntie Harper!" RJ giggled at her.

"Oh, I know, kiddo." Harper ruffled his hair playfully. "Did you see who was here?" She pointed to where Noah and Noel—Mia's twins—were sitting.

RJ squealed with happiness before he took off toward his friends. Mia hadn't been sure if she was going to make it or not, but I was happy to see my friend. She was still living up in Connecticut, but had plans to leave. I was hoping on convincing her to come to North Carolina. Maybe now that she was here, she could see how amazing it was.

"Do you want to go say hello?" Rand asked as we moved to sit down.

I smiled up at him. "I will, but right now I would love to get something to eat. I feel like I haven't eaten anything in days." Which was probably closer to the truth than I wanted to admit. "I'll have time after. It's our wedding day, baby," I whispered to him.

Rand placed his hand on my thigh as I sat down next to him. "You've made me the luckiest man in the world, Brooklyn. I'm going to spend the rest of my life showing you that." He kissed my lips lightly. "Along with fucking you every single chance I get." His eyes flashed with desire.

I felt warmth spread throughout my body. "Is that a promise, Rand?" I met his gaze.

"Damn fucking right."

"Hey, kids." Mason dropped into the chair next to Rand. "I—uh—need to get out of here." He glanced at me for a second before he looked at Rand. "Congratulations." He patted his friend on the shoulder. "Brooklyn, you look beautiful." He nodded at me.

I knew this had to do with London and speaking of—I glanced around the room. Where the fuck was she? Was this a wedding thing with them or what? I raised my eyebrows at Mason. "You have plans?" I took a sip of the wine that they had snuck into the building. "Or are you going to be fucking my sister again?"

Rand nearly spat his drink across the table. "Christ!" He wiped his mouth with the paper napkin in front of him. Then he realized why I asked. "Dude, could you maybe not this time?"

"I have no idea what you're talking about. Your sister is cute, but not my type." Mason stood up and nearly knocked the chair over. "I'll see you two later."

"Let him go, darlin'." Rand shook his head when I tried to get up.

"Why?"

"Mason is in love with your sister."

I felt all the color drain from my face as I sat back down. It made so much sense now that I thought about it. The way they both had been acting. Strange. Weird. Fucking whacked out of their minds. Mason and London?

"Oh, fuck." I wanted to slam my head against the table.

Rand snorted. "He's not a bad guy. He's probably just confused as all hell right now. Dude has never been in love in his life, but I totally get that. I had the same look probably until you showed up. Changed me."

"If he hurts her..."

"He won't," Rand assured me.

I brought the plastic cup of wine up to my mouth again as I watched Finn walk over to where Mia was standing with her twins who looked like they wanted to kill each other. I couldn't imagine having twins, one was hard enough. Not that RJ was a bad kid, but still. He kept me on my toes.

"Are you seeing that?" Rand whispered.

I was. The moment Finn started talking to Mia, she had turned so red she matched the roses on the cake she had made. Which reminded me—I had to ask her about maybe making a cake for RJ's birthday. She was so damn talented. Maybe I could get her to stay here and open her own bakery—the NASCAR family would help her with that.

"You're going to meddle, aren't you?" Rand teased me.

"I'm not—"

"Go on. Go see what's going on over there. I need to rest anyway." He looked exhausted.

"Baby, you want me to stay here? I should stay here. It's our wedding reception." I stroked Rand's cheek with the back of my hand.

He grabbed my hand only to bring it up to his lips. "Just

hurry back," he whispered softly.

Just as I went to stand up, I saw Finn move away from where Mia was talking to her boys—or rather I should say scolding them—or at least that is what it looked like. Then he walked over to where RJ was and squatted down to talk to him. Then Finn scooped my son up and walked back over to where Mia was. Then the next thing I knew all three boys ran off together like nothing was wrong.

Kids, right?

"I'll be damned," I muttered under my breath. "Hey, let's make a toast or something," I said to Rand.

"A toast?" Rand looked up at me like I had suddenly grown a second head.

I nodded. "Uh-huh. To thank everyone for coming. For doing all this. You know?" I kissed the top of his head. "Don't get up." I clapped my hands. "Hey!" My voice was clearly not loud enough, even when I tried to yell again.

"Hold up, darlin'," Rand roared next to me. "Do you think you could shut up for a second? My wife wants to talk to you!" He winked when I met his eyes. "I like calling you my wife." He chuckled softly.

I shook my head. "Always so damn subtle." I laced my fingers through his. "What my husband and I wanted to say was *thank you*. For everything." Rand dropped my hand so that he could wrap his arm around my waist. "You did way too much. We wanted to get married—" My voice cracked. "Shit, I didn't want to cry."

"Mama!" RJ cried from across the room.

"I know, baby. The swear jar." I dabbed at my eyes.

Rand squeezed me closer. "What Brooklyn wanted to say, or what we wanted to say, is that we really appreciate you. I've never had real friends before." He looked at me with love in his eyes. "Or a woman that made me want all of this. A family or friends—she changed my entire life the day we met. We were meant to be together and she was pretty much stuck with me the moment we had our first kiss," he teased.

"Not a lie," I admitted. "Again—you all did way more than you needed to and we thank you. From the bottom of our hearts." I leaned in to hug Rand lightly just as I saw London come back into the cafeteria with her dress a little too messy and she clearly looked like she had been crying.

I'll kill him.

"Don't." Rand shook his head. "Not today."

He was right. It was our wedding day.

"Let's dance," he suggested and held out his hand.

"Uh, you're in a wheelchair." I reminded him just as "Memories of Us" by Keith Urban began to play. It was like it was fate or something—I had always loved this song and thought about what a great wedding song it would be.

"I love you, darling." Rand whispered softly as I met his eyes. I know I've said that before and I'll spend the rest of my life saying it. Proving it, but I just want you to know. You are the best thing that has ever happened to me. You've made me a better man." He reached over to trace circles in my skin as the song played. "I wish—I wish I had gone after you that day and made you stay. Made you talk to me so that we could have worked things out, but that wasn't how it was supposed to be, was it? I'm okay with that now. It was rough, but I made it. I survived."

"Rand." I felt my throat close. I couldn't breathe. No one would ever know this man like I did. "I shouldn't have left and if I wasn't so fucking scared—" I closed my eyes as I held back tears. "For you to wait for me, you're damn crazy. I knew you were the one for me when you punched Travis." I giggled. "Why would someone who claimed to be this guy who didn't date do that? You tried to be this bad boy, but you weren't. You wanted someone who could settle you down and I got scared. Scared you would hurt me. So I hurt you first."

The truth.

"Well, guess what?" Rand tilted his head. "No one else can ever have me. I'm all *yours*. Until I'm an old, bald man." He snickered. "No more lies. No more of that shit. Ever again."

I nodded. "Never ever."

He pressed his lips to mine and I felt that kiss. Everywhere. In my mind. In my heart. In my goddamn soul.

Because just like Mason had said, Rand Shepard was my soul mate.

THE END

Acknowledgements

My amazing husband—I probably never, *ever* would have had the nerve to actually do this without you, my rock, my soulmate, *my everything*. Thank you for telling me I could do this, pushing me to do this and being my number one fan, but not in a creepy Annie Wilkes kind of way. You put up with my crazy bullshit even though I truly don't deserve you. I must have done something right somewhere to have been blessed with you in my life. *Real love is forever.*

Stephanie—I hope you know now this means you're going to have to read everything going forward and be my beta reader. Thanks for being my very own Harper and I'm sure it won't surprise you that her original name was Bobbie. Every single best friend I write about is always you, no matter what. Thank you for being my person, be frie.

My family—Thank you for acting like you want to read this book. I kid of course, but I know you're trying to be supportive. Mom, just skip over the sex stuff because I know you have never done anything like that before.

Alicia over at Inkitt—You might love Rand more than Brooklyn, but we won't tell her. You were such a huge supporter when I was writing this and it meant more to me than you know.

I hope that you like the updated version just as much. The others are getting their books, too.

ellie at My Brother's Editor—I appreciate your hard work and for putting up with me. This job cannot be easy and you are the bee's knees, the cat's whiskers, the monkey's eyebrows—well you get it. I hope to be able to do this again and again as long as people actually like my shit.

You for reading this—Thank you so much for taking a chance on me! If you have the time to leave an honest review that would mean the world to me.

Until next time,
Sundae

Reach Out

All things Sundae Leighton

(new releases, teasers, sneak peaks, email list, social club):

http://www.sundaeleighton.com

Facebook Readers Group:

http://www.facebook.com/groups/233608387885905/

Facebook:

http://www.facebook.com/authorsundaeleighton

Instagram: http://www.instagram.com/sundaeleighton/

Twitter: http://www.twitter.com/sundaeleighton

Facebook:

http://www.facebook.com/authorsundaeleighton

Goodreads:

http://www.goodreads.com/authorsundaeleighton

www.ingramcontent.com/pod-product-compliance
Lightning Source LLC
Chambersburg PA
CBHW021139110726
47900CB00002B/423